DEATH AT THE FEAST

A KIPPER COTTAGE MYSTERY

JAN DURHAM

INKUBATOR
BOOKS

Published by Inkubator Books
www.inkubatorbooks.com

Copyright © 2022 by Jan Durham

ISBN (Paperback): 978-1-915275-64-6
ISBN (eBook): 978-1-915275-63-9
ISBN (Hardback): 978-1-915275-65-3

Jan Durham has asserted her right to be identified as the author of this work.

DEATH AT THE FEAST is a work of fiction. People, places, events, and situations are the product of the author's imagination. Any resemblance to actual persons, living or dead is entirely coincidental.

1

'I hate mulled wine.'

'That's ridiculous. No one hates mulled wine.'

'I do.' Liz McLuckie grimaced. 'It tastes like medicine.'

'Not when it's made properly,' Mags finished, filling her muslin bag with spices. Pushing her dark fringe out of her eyes, she wiped her hands on her apron. 'The trick is not to use too many cloves.'

'I thought cloves were the whole point?'

'Not at all. I use all kinds of things. Cinnamon. Cranberries. Star anise. Then, when it's all in the pan, I add the lemons. Pity you're not going to the mayor's party, or you could try it.' Mags's face crinkled. She groped in her apron pocket for a tissue and sneezed into it.

'Spices up your nose?' suggested Liz.

Mags shook her head. 'A cold. Just my luck, getting one for Christmas.'

'Liz!' The distant voice was imperious. 'I need you!'

Liz hurried out of the kitchen, along the corridor stacked with cash-and-carry boxes and crates of vegetables, and through the beaded curtain into the main part of the café. To her alarm she saw Grazyna, Mags's statuesque assistant manager, teetering on a ladder, trying to put a star on top of the newly decorated Christmas tree.

'Couldn't you have waited two seconds?' Liz hurried to steady the ladder, and watched as Grazyna placed the star on the top. 'You'll kill yourself.'

Grazyna ignored her. 'There,' she said as she climbed back down the steps. 'It looks quite good, yes?'

'Yes.'

It looked very good. The tree had pride of place in the Dickensian window of the Full Moon Café. Before Mags and her wife, Tilly, had bought the café, it used to be a chip shop, with stainless steel fittings caked with cooking fat and grease stains on the ceiling. It looked very different now. There was an old-fashioned bookshop at one end, specialising in New Age subjects – spiritualism, Tarot cards and self-help – and a spiral staircase that led up to a reading nook, complete with battered leather chairs. The other end of the room was set up with tables and a big pine counter showcasing home-made cakes. It was all decorated with a wildly eclectic assortment of antiques – melamine tables mixed with wooden ones, lava lamps with old-fashioned fringed standing lamps and a neon sign that said 'Stardust'. It should have looked like a junk-yard, but didn't. It looked magical. The Christmas tree and strings of fairy lights only added to the effect.

'Shall I switch the tree lights on?' asked Liz.

'In a minute.' Grazyna glanced at one of the tables, where her ten-year-old twins, Lukasz and Eryk, had their heads together, making paper chains. 'I do not want to distract them.' She leaned in to Liz and whispered, 'The chains look like shit, but it has kept them quiet for an hour.'

Liz grinned. Grazyna's English was very good, but the niceties of vocabulary often escaped her. Liz had to agree, however, that peaceful moments were rare with the twins and should definitely be savoured.

'I might even manage to make a cup of tea.' Grazyna smiled at Liz. Her habitual demeanour was stern – she usually looked like she was about to punch somebody – but when she smiled, it brightened her whole face. Liz liked to see Grazyna smile. She'd had a hard life.

'There, I think that's everything.' Mags bustled through the curtain, with her coat on, a cardboard box in her arms and her bag slung over one shoulder. 'Are you sure you're okay to lock up, Grazyna?'

'Of course.' Grazyna sniffed. 'I have done it a hundred times.'

'Excellent.' Mags was used to Grazyna's snarkiness and immune to it. 'Then I'll see you tomorrow.'

The café door opened with a tinkle, and a head with cropped, bleached blonde hair poked inside. It was accompanied by a waft of patchouli.

'What's keeping you, woman?' cried Tilly as she came into the café. 'I've been waiting out there for hours.' Tilly, bright and impetuous, was *yang* to Mags's *yin*. She was wearing a combination of a leather jacket and a floaty Indian skirt that should have looked odd, but just looked achingly cool.

'You have not,' said Mags mildly. 'You've only been in the van five minutes.' She reached the door; then she stopped. Her eyes widened. 'The tempura batter! It's still in the fridge!' She thrust the box she was carrying at Tilly and disappeared back through the curtain into the kitchen. Tilly shook her head, making her feather earrings flutter.

'You do know it starts at eight?' she called after Mags. She looked at Liz and Grazyna. 'It'll be a bloody miracle if we get there before Christmas.' Then she spotted the tree. 'Ohhhhh. That's lovely. Good job, Grazyna.'

'Thank you.'

Mags reappeared with a large Tupperware container and watched as Tilly opened the door.

'Don't drop that box,' she said. 'That's all my oils and dipping sauces. If you drop it, I'll have to start from scratch.'

'Then I'll do my best not to drop it,' said Tilly with a wink. She tucked it under one arm as she held the door open for Mags. 'Have a good time at B's, Liz. Tell me all about it tomorrow. All about her.'

'I will.'

'I hope she's nice.'

'So do I.'

'Come on, Tilly,' called Mags from the street. 'You'll make us late!'

Tilly pulled a face of mock outrage and followed.

When they'd gone, Liz helped Grazyna sweep the floor clean of stray pine needles and bits of tinsel. Just as they finished, the boys lifted their heads from the table, like synchronised, spiky-headed meerkats.

'The tree!'

'Let's switch on the lights!'

'And do a Christmas dance!'

'And put up our chains!'

'What are we going to put them up with?'

'Have we got any drawing pins, Mum?'

'Or tape?'

Grazyna met Liz's eye. So much for her cup of tea.

THE AIR OUTSIDE WAS CRISP, and the cobbles were treacherous underfoot. Liz carried her bottle of wine carefully. She didn't want to slip and drop it and turn up at Benedict's empty-handed. She tiptoed gingerly down Sandgate, the narrow, cobbled heart of the fishing town of Whitby, lined with small independent shops selling souvenirs, books, ice cream and handmade jewellery. Even though it was dark, there were still quite a few people out and about, making the most of the extended Christmas shopping hours. All the shopkeepers had made an effort with their decorations, many of them in Victorian style, that made the street look like a scene straight out of Dickens.

When she emerged from Sandgate, she turned right, onto the harbour, towards the swing bridge that crossed the River Esk and led to the more modern part of town. The bridge was up, so Liz had to wait with the other pedestrians as a fishing boat passed through to the marina. While she waited, she watched the twinkling reflections on the North Sea as it swirled below. The sea itself looked thick and glassy, and Liz wondered if the harbour had ever actually frozen.

The winter weather was very different to Liz's childhood memories of the town. In the school holidays she and her sister used to make the long drive from Edinburgh in her father's rickety old work van. They would spend warm days on the beach and amusements, eating fish and chips and exploring the cobbled yards and alleyways. In winter it felt very different. The salty air was frozen, with all the scents of sea and fish and fast food locked away. Tonight, even the usually raucous herring gulls were silent.

The bell rang, and the barrier on the bridge lifted. Liz continued on her way.

As she passed New Quay Plaza, she admired the huge Norwegian spruce tree that was sprinkled with lights. It had attracted a few admiring families and a trio of carol singers who were singing 'Away in a Manger'. Liz recognised the tall figure of choirmaster Gregory Willis and two other members of her choir, the Eskside Singers. She waved to them as she passed, and gave the tree one last approving look. She'd decided not to put up a tree in her own cottages this year.

Decorating for Christmas always seemed rather dispiriting without her husband, Mark. It was astonishing to think he'd been dead for almost five years.

Liz had come to Whitby shortly after he died. After renting for a couple of years on the West Cliff, she had bought two fishermen's cottages on the East Cliff. It was her intention to do them both up, then rent one out to holiday-makers and live in the other. It was an ambitious project to take on at fifty years old, and things hadn't exactly gone to plan. She'd managed to renovate one – Kipper Cottage – restoring the stone flags under the hideous swirly carpets and even finding the original inglenook fireplace behind faux wood cladding. Unfortunately, a fire at Halloween had undone a lot of her good work, and it would take a while to get Kipper ready for guests again. In the meantime, she was sleeping in Gull Cottage next door, which still had its hideous carpets and wood cladding. She'd barely started the renovations there.

Liz's friend, Benedict, an ex-Navy man, lived in a tall house near the botanical gardens of Pannet Park, known by locals as the posh part of town. The houses were a mix of Georgian and Edwardian, very different from the higgledy-piggledy cottages in the old town where she lived. His house was set back from the road behind a tall hedge. As she opened the gate and went up the path, she saw the path had been salted, and light shone from many of the big sash windows. The porch light was on above the door, and the shrubs beside the door had fairy lights strung through them. Clearly, Benedict hadn't let being a widower dampen *his* festive spirit.

She rang the bell.

Benedict answered almost immediately. He looked flustered, his short silver hair sticking up in spikes, and his lean frame wrapped in an apron that said 'Galley Slave'. In spite of his age – he was a couple of years older than Liz – he still had a boyish demeanour. As soon as he opened the door, he headed back to the kitchen.

'You don't need to ring, you know. You can just come straight in.'

'Really?' Liz hadn't realised they'd reached that level of friendship.

'And if the door's locked, there's a key under the hydrangea.'

'Okay.' She tried to ignore the security implications of that, took off her coat, petted a couple of cats that had come to greet her, and followed him into the kitchen. The kitchen was large but welcoming, with chunky cabinets, a butler's sink, and the Aga stove that was always on, even in summer. The table was littered with dirty bowls, flour and discarded utensils.

'I'm a bit out of my depth,' admitted Benedict. 'Kevin tells me Anna's vegan. I thought I'd make a vegan mushroom wellington, but I've been having trouble with the pastry.'

'Oh?' Liz tried to sound interested. She liked to eat food, and Benedict's food in particular, but she wasn't a cook and wasn't in the least bit curious about culinary endeavours.

'It should have gone in the oven twenty minutes ago, and I haven't even had a shower yet.' He gave his pastry parcel one final tuck, then opened the Aga door and slid it inside.

He groaned. 'The potatoes are in. But I still have the salad to make.'

'Tell you what,' said Liz, 'why don't you go shower, and I'll do the salad? Even I can manage that.'

'You're a star!' Benedict grinned and kissed her on the forehead. 'Everything's in the fridge.'

Liz blushed to the roots of her hair as he hurried out. It had been a very brotherly kiss, but the first time he'd actually touched her with affection. She gave herself a shake. She was being ridiculous – a fifty-year-old woman acting like a teenager. She'd only realised how she felt about Benedict a few months before, in the summer. When Mark had died, Liz had genuinely thought her heart had died with him, and that the romantic part of her life was over forever. But gradually, as she'd got to know Benedict, she'd found that wasn't true. It had been a huge and not altogether welcome surprise when she'd finally had to admit to herself that what she felt for him was more than friendship. Unfortunately, that realisation had coincided with him starting to date Gillian Garraway, their local reverend. The romance hadn't lasted long, but Liz suspected that Benedict still had feelings for Gillian. It was getting harder and harder for Liz to hide her own.

She found the salad stuff in the fridge, washed the rocket and coriander, and chopped spring onions, while Benedict's many cats made a point of ignoring her. The cats were a legacy from Benedict's late wife, Kate, who had never been able to resist a stray. When Liz had first started coming to the house, they'd been hostile, probably because they could smell Nelson, her English bull terrier. But as they'd grown used to her, she'd gradually become part of their scenery. Much as she had with Benedict.

She sighed, dumped the salad into a big glass bowl, and started to clean up the mess Benedict had left on the table. She heard the front door open.

'Hello?' called Kevin.

Liz dried her hands and hurried through to the hall.

Kevin, Benedict's son, was tall and wholesome looking, with the freshly scrubbed air of a schoolboy. The petite woman he'd brought with him had very pale skin and a sprinkling of freckles, wearing jeans and a red coat that clashed gloriously with her red hair.

'This is Anna.'

Liz hurriedly finished drying her hands on her jeans and stretched out her hand. 'I'm Liz.'

Anna nodded shyly.

'Where's Dad?' Kevin hung up his coat, then helped Anna with hers.

'Having a shower. He's running a bit late. He's been having trouble with his pastry.'

Anna flashed a worried look at Kevin.

'His <u>vegan</u> pastry,' said Liz.

Kevin and Anna both looked relieved. 'I did tell him,' said Kevin, 'but I wasn't sure he'd remember.'

'We're having mushroom wellington.'

'Sounds lovely,' said Anna. Her voice was low and musical.

Liz decided she liked her.

THE MUSHROOM WELLINGTON was up to Benedict's usual standards, even if Liz's salad lacked finesse. As their bottle of red wine disappeared, Anna's shyness melted. She told them about her job as assistant pathologist to the coroner in Scarborough. She and Kevin, a police detective, had met at work a couple of months earlier while he was investigating the mysterious death of journalist Donnie Satterthwaite.

'Such a horrible way to die,' said Anna. She looked at Liz. 'Kevin tells me <u>you</u> caught the murderer?'

'Not just me.' Liz blushed. 'We all had a hand in it.' She decided to change the subject. 'Did you say there was pudding, Benedict?'

'Lemon mousse. Does everybody want some?'

'Definitely!' said Kevin.

'Yes, please.' Anna nodded.

Benedict headed for the kitchen, followed by Liz. They huddled by the open refrigerator door.

'She seems very nice,' whispered Liz.

'She does, doesn't she? Far too good for him.' Benedict grinned. He was joking, of course.

'They seem to have a lot in common,' said Liz.

A shadow passed over Benedict's face. When Gillian had broken things off with him, she'd told him it was because they had nothing in common, but Liz knew there was more to it than that. She could have kicked herself for reopening the wound.

The awkward moment was interrupted by sudden banging on the front door.

'Who on earth...?' said Benedict. He and Liz both had two glasses of lemon mousse in their hands. Not content with just pounding on the door, the mysterious caller then also rang the bell.

'Whoever it is,' said Liz, 'they're persistent.'

Benedict and Liz shoved the glasses on the table and hurried into the hall just as Kevin and Anna also appeared. Benedict opened the door.

It was Tilly and Mags, both looking distraught. Tilly had her arm around Mags, supporting her, and Benedict helped Tilly guide her to a chair. Mags blew her nose and wiped her eyes with a tissue. She couldn't speak.

'Is she okay?' Benedict asked Tilly. 'What on earth's happened?'

Tilly just shook her head, apparently also lost for words. Liz frowned. That wasn't like her at all.

Mags looked up at Benedict tearfully. 'It's the mayor,' she sobbed. 'I think I've killed him!'

2

'A sesame allergy?' echoed Benedict.

They were all in the kitchen, surrounded by dirty dinner dishes and abandoned glasses of lemon mousse.

'A really bad one.' Tilly nodded. 'His wife warned us about it when she booked us to do the catering.'

'I didn't put sesame seeds in anything!' wailed Mags. 'I was so careful.'

'So how did it happen?' asked Kevin.

'We have no idea,' said Tilly. 'But there must have been sesame in something. He just keeled over.'

'It was awful,' sobbed Mags. 'He couldn't breathe.'

'Didn't anyone have an EpiPen?' asked Anna.

Tilly nodded. 'His wife, Carolyn, had one in her bag. She injected him, but it made no difference. When the ambulance arrived, they tried to defibrillate him, but...' Tilly tailed off.

'Is he...?' Liz didn't want to finish her sentence either.

'We don't know,' said Tilly. 'The ambulance took him to hospital. But it really didn't look good.' She turned to Benedict. 'Sorry for just turning up, B, but I didn't want to take her home like this.'

'You did the right thing.' Benedict patted her shoulder and poured Mags some tea from the pot. He added two spoonfuls of sugar.

'Good for shock,' he said.

Anna looked at her watch and stood up. 'I'm really sorry,' she said. 'But I have to be going. I have a ridiculously early shift in the morning.'

'I'll run you home,' said Kevin. 'Then I'll ring the station and the hospital and see if anyone can tell me anything.'

'Thanks,' said Tilly.

Kevin and Anna headed for the door.

'Nice to meet you, Anna,' said Mags. 'I don't suppose you want to take a doggy bag home?' It was an attempt at a joke, but it came out in a sob.

Tilly explained, 'We've brought all the food back with us. We couldn't just leave it there for the museum to clean up.'

'I wouldn't get rid of any of it if I were you,' said Kevin. 'Just in case.'

'Just in case I've poisoned the mayor!' A fresh burst of sobbing came from Mags. Tilly put her arm around her as Kevin and Anna headed out.

'What are we going to do with all that food?' wailed Mags.

'Why don't we bring it in here for now,' suggested Benedict. 'There's plenty of room in the conservatory. Liz will give me a hand, won't you?'

'Of course.'

'You two stay here, where it's warm,' said Benedict. 'It won't take us long.'

Liz and Benedict bundled themselves into their coats and went out. Tilly had practically abandoned the van; it was parked with its wheels on the pavement outside the gate.

'Careful,' said Benedict. 'It's icy here.'

He unlocked the van and opened the back doors. A delicious aroma wafted out. There were trays of food stacked inside: hors d'oeuvres, tempura chicken and prawn, sausage rolls and sandwiches. Liz and Benedict stared at the feast in dismay.

'I don't suppose anyone can eat it now,' said Liz, her stomach rumbling even though she'd only just eaten.

'Best not, I suppose.'

They unloaded the van, carrying trays into the house. It took several trips backwards and forwards until all that was left was Mags's box of sauces and oils.

'There's a handbag in here too,' said Benedict. He showed Liz a green velvet evening bag with a diamanté chain.

'Nice,' said Liz. 'It must belong to Tilly or Mags. Better leave it in there for now. I'll lock the van.'

Back in the conservatory, Liz and Benedict surveyed the trays of food on the conservatory table.

'Such a shame,' said Liz.

Benedict looked at the box of sauces and oils he had put on the table. He pulled one of the jars from the box and inspected the dark liquid through the glass. He opened the lid and sniffed it. His eyes widened.

'What?' asked Liz.

Benedict just stared at her.

'What?' she prompted.

'I really hate to say this... but I think this is sesame oil.'

Liz frowned, took the jar and sniffed it. 'I think you're right. But surely...?'

Benedict nodded, appalled. 'What should we do?'

'I suppose we should tell Mags?'

Benedict didn't look too thrilled at the prospect, but nodded all the same.

They went into the kitchen, where Mags and Tilly were chatting quietly.

Mags frowned when she saw the jar Liz was carrying. 'What are you doing with that?'

'I'm not sure,' said Liz. 'What's in it?'

'The oil I fried the tempura in.'

'Are you sure?'

'Of course I'm sure.'

Liz and Benedict exchanged a look.

'What's going on?' Mags took the jar from Liz and sniffed it. She scowled, blew her nose vigorously into a tissue, then sniffed it again. An expression of horror crept over her face.

'Oh my God. I fried all the tempura in this. But... I don't understand. I filled it myself this afternoon, with vegetable oil and soy.'

'You couldn't have made a mistake?' asked Liz. 'You do have a cold.'

'No. I swear. I did have sesame oil in the café, but I was careful not to go anywhere near it. I definitely didn't put that in there.' Mags put her hands over her face. 'Oh God, this is horrible!' Tilly took Benedict and Liz to one side and spoke in a whisper.

'If she says it's supposed to be vegetable oil, I believe her.'

'So what happened?' asked Liz.

Tilly shook her head. 'I have no idea.'

'You know you're going to have to tell the police?' said Benedict.

'I know.' Tilly frowned. 'But I don't want to spell that out to Mags just now. I just want to get her home.'

LIZ GOT a lift back in the van with Tilly and Mags as far as the café, then walked home to Henrietta Street. It was only a five-minute walk, but Liz took her time. She loved Whitby at night, when she had the narrow streets to herself. Her feet crunching on frost underfoot. The stars, sharp in the velvet sky, were doing their best to outdo the lights in the shop windows. Liz took some deep breaths and tried to organise her thoughts. Poor Mags. She'd really taken the events of the evening to heart. What if the mayor died? It was too awful to think about.

When she reached the door of Gull Cottage, she put her key in the lock.

Yip, yip, yip!

Nelson, the English bull terrier, called joyously to her through the door and hurled himself against it on the other side. She had trouble pushing it open.

'Get in, you daftie!' She caught the bouncing dog and rubbed his ears.

'I wasn't gone too long, was I? Did you miss me?'

The wildly wagging stump of his tail told her he had. He was an odd-looking animal, with a huge coffin-shaped head that seemed far too big for his stocky body, and a patch over one eye that gave him a raffish, piratical air. Certain unkind people had dubbed him the 'ugliest dog in Yorkshire', but Liz disagreed. To her, he was perfect. She hugged him, and he looked at her expectantly.

'I suppose you want to go out for a pee now?'

He wagged his stumpy tail. It didn't matter what else might be going on in the world – distraught friends, potentially dead mayors or anything else – there were still some things that had to be taken care of.

THE NEXT DAY, as soon as she was up and about, Liz tried to ring Tilly, but her call went straight to answerphone. Then she tried Kevin, and the same thing happened. She put down her mobile phone, exasperated. Was the mayor okay? It was still too early to buy the local newspaper, the *Whitby Bugle*.

She was just about to put the kettle on when she heard

distant whistling out in the street – 'God Rest Ye Merry Gentlemen'. Her spirits lifted. There was something even more reliable than the *Bugle* – or rather *someone*. She pushed her feet into her wellies and flung on her coat, then went outside.

'Morning, Mrs Mac.' Mike, the fishmonger, clad in his high-vis vest, was dragging his usual tray of herring to the smokehouse next door. Liz could tell they already had the fires lit, waiting for him – the scent of woodsmoke hung heavily in the frosty air.

Mike pursed his lips. 'Terrible news about Neil Grogan. He was just fifty-five, you know. Same age as me. A man in his prime.'

Liz didn't like the sound of that past tense. 'He's not...?'

'As a doornail. A nut allergy, apparently. It happened at the council party last night.'

Poor Mags.

'Still,' said Mike philosophically, 'we've all got to go some time, I suppose.'

'Would you like a cuppa when you've dropped that off?'

'Not this morning, if you don't mind. I still have most of my deliveries to make. I had trouble getting the van started this morning. Some other time, though, eh?'

'It's a promise. See you later.'

She went back inside, glad Mike had turned down her offer – she needed to get to the café and find out if Mags and Tilly had heard the news. But first she had to get dressed and take Nelson for a proper walk.

THE CLIMB up to St Mary's churchyard and the ruined abbey on the clifftop never failed to raise Liz's spirits, even though it was hard going. One hundred and ninety-nine stone steps led up the cliffside, worn smooth over the centuries, every tenth step featuring a small brass disc with a Roman numeral that told you how far you'd come. This morning the steps were particularly slippery, and Liz had to rein in Nelson, who was eagerly trying to pull her up them. She stopped as usual on one of the coffin steps, so called because they were made deeper, for pallbearers to rest on their way up to the church. She paused to catch her breath and take in the view.

The old town lay jumbled below her, its usually red-tiled roofs white with frost, and smoke rising vertically from dozens of chimney pots. It was a view she liked to imagine hadn't changed for three centuries, with only the sprinkling of TV aerials and satellite dishes betraying the fact she hadn't somehow stepped back in time. When she'd got her breath back, Liz allowed Nelson to pull her up the rest of the steps.

At St Caedmon's Cross, at the top of the cliff, Liz took the left-hand path that led into St Mary's graveyard. She let Nelson off the lead and followed him along the clifftop path. It was her habit now to avert her eyes from the spot among the gravestones where she and Nelson had found the body of Professor Ian Crowby the summer before, and from the repaired section of fence that ran along the cliff, where she had almost fallen to her death not long afterwards. Instead, she stood well back from the edge of the cliff and took in the vertiginous view down onto Henrietta Street. She could clearly see the roofs of her own cottages below. She blinked. Was she imagining it, or were there some tiles missing on Gull's roof? The missing tiles all seemed to be in one spot. Had something come down from the clifftop – a loose rock, perhaps? If so, that wasn't unusual. She sighed. It was just something else to add to the long list of things that needed fixing.

After their clifftop walk, Liz took Nelson back down the steps and along Church Street to Sandgate. The Full Moon Café wasn't open yet, but she could see Grazyna inside, putting fresh cakes into the display case on the counter. Liz tapped on the window, and Grazyna came to open the door.

'It's only you,' she said. 'I suppose you had better come in.'

'And a very good morning to you too,' said Liz, with a smile. She unclipped Nelson from his lead, and he ran off to find the plastic pig Mags kept for him behind the counter. 'Are they up yet?'

'They are at the police station.'

'What?'

'Telling the police about the sesame oil they found in the van.'

'Ah.'

'Stupid,' muttered Grazyna.

'You think they should have kept quiet about it?'

'Don't you? It does not look good, especially for someone like Mags.'

Liz had to admit Grazyna was right. Mags and Tilly had both been in trouble with the police before. In fact, they'd met in a young offenders institution. Tilly had been there for burglary. Liz wasn't sure why Mags had been there, but whatever the reason, she could do without coming to the attention of the police again.

'Do they know the mayor's dead?' asked Liz.

Grazyna nodded. 'Kevin called them last night. They have not taken it well.'

Liz could imagine. Grazyna looked at her watch and sighed.

Liz took the hint. 'Do you need a hand to open up?'

'That would be good, thank you. Could you please put out the clean cutlery while I switch on the coffee machine?'

Grazyna had just disappeared into the kitchen to fill the coffee jug when someone banged on the door. Through the glass, Liz could see it was a woman, probably in her early thirties, with blonde highlights and a tan, wearing an expensive ski jacket. Liz hurried to open the door. Now she was closer, the woman looked less polished – there were wisps of hair escaping from her ponytail, and mascara streaked under her eyes.

'I'm sorry, we're not open yet,' said Liz. 'If you'd like to come back in—'

'Where are they?'

'Who?'

'Margaret and Matilda.'

Liz wasn't used to hearing Mags and Tilly called by their proper names. 'I'm afraid they're' – she hesitated, not wanting to say exactly where they were – 'out.'

'Hiding from me, I suppose.'

Liz frowned. 'Why would they do that?'

'I'm Carolyn Grogan.'

Liz's eyes widened. 'The mayor's wife?'

'The mayor's *widow*.'

Liz took a deep breath. 'You'd better come in.'

3

Carolyn Grogan lifted her chin and marched into the café. Nelson abandoned his plastic pig and came to greet her. Carolyn ignored him.

'Mags and Tilly honestly aren't here,' said Liz. Carolyn was much younger than she had expected. Hadn't Mike said that Neil Grogan was in his fifties?

'So you say.' Carolyn glared pointedly at the beaded curtain that led to the kitchen. They could both hear running water.

'Would you like me to give them a message?'

'Yes.' Carolyn turned her furious, bleak gaze on Liz. 'You can tell them they'll be hearing from me. And from my solicitor. I'm going to tell everyone in town that they killed my poor Neil. And I'm going to sue them for every penny they have.' She turned, almost tripping over Nelson, who was standing behind her. She swept him roughly out of the way with her foot and stomped out the door.

Liz and Nelson looked at each other. Grazyna appeared through the curtain, wiping her hands on a tea towel.

'Did I hear someone come in?' she said.

'Carolyn Grogan.'

Grazyna's eyes widened. 'Shit.'

This time Liz couldn't argue with Grazyna's vocabulary.

MAGS AND TILLY appeared about an hour later. The café was quite busy, but Grazyna waved them into the kitchen, insisting she could manage on her own. Liz followed.

'How did it go?' she asked.

Tilly helped Mags take off her coat.

'Not great,' she said. 'I don't think anyone believes Mags didn't use the sesame oil carelessly.'

'Who took your statement?'

'Bill Williams.'

'That's good.' Detective Constable Bill Williams, known to his fellow officers as Double Bill, gave a very good impression of being dim, but Liz knew he was actually a lot sharper than most of his colleagues. He also had a big heart. She didn't think he'd let Mags incriminate herself inadvertently.

'But,' added Tilly, 'we ran into Flint on our way out.'

Liz winced. Detective Inspector Flint had only been in Whitby since the spring, but Liz had already tangled with her on quite a few, very painful, occasions. 'What did she say?'

'She said there would have to be an inquest.'

'I suppose that's normal, with a sudden death?'

'I suppose so.'

Mags put her head in her hands. Liz and Tilly looked at each other helplessly. Then Tilly's gaze fell on something hanging on the back of one of the chairs.

'I should try to find out who that belongs to.'

It was the green velvet evening bag.

'I saw it in the van last night,' said Liz. 'I thought it was yours.'

Tilly shook her head. 'We picked it up with all our other

stuff by accident. I should take it back to the museum in case someone's looking for it.'

'Give it to me,' said Liz. 'You have enough on your plate already.'

Her words made Tilly groan. 'The food! It's still at Benedict's, isn't it? Flint said we could get rid of everything except the sesame oil. She wants us to take that into the station.'

Mags lifted her head from her hands. She looked utterly exhausted. Tilly's forehead creased with concern.

'Why don't you have a lie-down, love? I can manage everything here.'

Mags nodded, kissed Tilly on the cheek and headed out. Liz listened to her going up the stairs to the flat and, when she was sure she was out of earshot, leaned towards Tilly.

'Carolyn Grogan was here.'

'What?'

'About an hour ago.'

'What did she say?'

'I don't think you want to know.'

Tilly caught Liz's hand, her eyes brimming with sudden tears. 'Oh, Liz, I don't think it's going to be a very merry Christmas.'

'God rest ye merry gentlemen, let nothing you dismay

'For Jesus Christ our saviour was born on Christmas day...'

Gregory tapped his baton on his music stand. Everyone stopped singing. The piano tinkled to a halt.

'Tenors, don't forget that little lift at the beginning of the second line... *Fo-or*. Ladies, you'll have to give the gents a bit of space to do that.'

Liz caught Benedict's eye on the other side of the room. He winked.

'Don't go rushing into that line too fast. It's not a race.' Gregory turned to the pianist. 'Can we slow it down just a little, Crystal?'

'Sorry, I'm a bit rusty.' Crystal grimaced. She taught wood-working at Whitby Academy and had a heavy touch on the keys. Their usual piano player was Deborah Grogan, who ran the Museum of Whitby Jet and was also Neil Grogan's ex-wife. Unsurprisingly, she hadn't turned up for practice. In a small town like Whitby, the death of one person tended to affect everyone, one way or another, like a stone tossed into a pond.

'Okay.' Gregory tapped his baton. 'Back to the beginning, please.'

They started again.

'God rest ye merry gentlemen...'

Liz surrendered to the music. She had a decent voice, but unfortunately it fell somewhere between soprano and contralto. She never felt entirely comfortable singing either part – it was too much of a strain at the top of the soprano range, and too much of a struggle at the bottom of contralto. But she enjoyed it, which she supposed was really the point. Her choir, the Eskside Singers, had just increased their meetings at the church hall from once to three times a week. They were rehearsing for the St Mary's Christmas Eve service.

As they were singing, the door opened, and two figures entered. Liz recognised Irwin Gladwell and his elderly mum, Iris. She waved enthusiastically to them both as they took off their coats. Irwin, a bachelor in his early forties was wearing a shirt, tie, and a particularly natty Christmas jumper.

When everyone had finished the song, Irwin approached Gregory.

'Mr Willis? We spoke on the phone.' He shook Gregory's hand. 'Irwin and Iris Gladwell. Sorry we're late. I thought you started at eight.'

'No worries. I'm just delighted you're both here. Another tenor is particularly welcome. I don't know why us gentlemen are so shy about singing.' They smiled at each other. 'Can either of you read music?' Both Gladwells shook their heads.

'Oh well, it's Christmas carols, so I daresay you know them anyway.' Gregory beamed at Iris. 'Let's try you in the sopranos to start, shall we? Can you please keep an eye on Mrs Gladwell, Lucy?' He shepherded Iris to sit beside his lead soprano, while Irwin found a seat beside Benedict. Gregory took a deep breath and picked up his baton again.

'Okay. Thank you, Crystal, whenever you're ready.'

Crystal played the intro.

'God rest ye merry gentlemen...'

'GOD REST YE MERRY GENTLEMEN...'

Crystal broke off in alarm. Stranded without the piano, everyone else stuttered to a halt. They all stared, round-eyed, at Iris.

'Good heavens,' said Gregory. 'You have a very powerful voice, Mrs Gladwell.'

'THANK YOU.'

Iris was well known among her friends for being unable to speak at anything less than a bellow. When Liz had first met her, she'd thought it might be because the old lady was deaf, but that turned out not to be the case. Apparently she'd spoken like that all her life. Clearly, she sang like that too. Gregory's eyes slid to Irwin, who was finding the ceiling particularly interesting.

'Okay,' said Gregory. 'Let's start again. Maybe try to dial it down just a notch, Mrs Gladwell, if that's okay?'

'OKAY.'

Gregory nodded at Crystal, who began again.

'God rest ye merry gentlemen, let nothing you dismay.'

'GOD REST YE MERRY GENTLEMEN, LET NOTHING YOU DISMAY.'

'For Jesus Christ our saviour was born on Christmas day...'

'FOR JESUS CHRIST OUR SAVIOUR WAS BORN ON CHRISTMAS DAY...'

If Iris had 'dialled it down a notch', it wasn't obvious. Somehow everyone stumbled through to the end of the carol. Liz noticed that quite a few people had put a finger in whichever of their ears was closest to Iris. When they'd finished, Gregory put down his baton. He looked like a bird that had flown into a window.

'Thank you,' he said. He hesitated. 'You know what, I think we'll leave it there for tonight. See you all again on Thursday.'

'IS THAT IT?' huffed Iris. 'I WOULDN'T HAVE BOTHERED COMING IF I'D KNOWN IT WAS JUST FOR ONE SONG.'

BACK AT GULL COTTAGE, after she'd taken Nelson for his evening walk, Liz changed into her pyjamas and made herself a mug of cocoa. She sat at the kitchen table and tried not to let the patterned carpet and ugly faux wood panelling irritate her. She would start renovations at Gull as soon as she'd made good the fire damage in Kipper and had some rental income coming in again. In the meantime, she just had to adopt a Zen state of mind... and get a roofer to look at the missing slates.

The green evening bag caught her eye. She'd brought it home from the café and had rung the museum that afternoon to see if anyone had been asking for it, but no one had. She picked it up and tipped the contents onto the table.

There was a twenty-pound note, three pound coins, and a lipstick – Chanel's Rouge Noir. Expensive, like the bag. There was also a taxi receipt for Colin's Cabs. The ink on the writing was smudged, so Liz wasn't able to decipher the fare. There was no clue to the bag's owner, which was frustrating. She made a mental note to ring Colin's Cabs in the morning to see if they had a record of who they'd taken to the museum. Failing that, she would have to take the bag to the police station. She put everything back in the bag and sipped her cocoa.

It had been an eventful couple of days. She believed Mags one hundred per cent when she said she'd prepared nut-free oils and sauces for the party. Someone had swapped the vegetable oil for sesame oil at the museum.

But who would do such a thing?

4

'Who would want Neil Grogan dead?'

'That's the million-dollar question, isn't it?' said Kevin. 'Assuming Mags didn't make a mistake.'

'What does everyone think at the station?' asked Liz.

'That Mags made a mistake.'

'What do *you* think?'

Kevin eyed his bacon sandwich thoughtfully. 'If it was anyone but her, I'd agree. But I just can't see Mags being careless.'

'Me neither,' agreed Liz. 'So that only really leaves one possibility.'

'Someone swapped the oil.' Kevin took a huge bite of his sandwich and chewed thoughtfully. He often took his lunch with Liz, either at Gull Cottage or in their favourite all-weather shelter looking out over the sea on the West Cliff. It was too cold today for lunch *al fresco*, so he had joined her in the swirly-carpeted, wood-panelled warmth of her kitchen. He swallowed his sandwich, then washed it down with a gulp of tea.

'I suppose I'd be wasting my breath telling you not to get involved?' he said. 'Again.'

'This one's different. Mags is our friend.'

Kevin gave her a resigned look.

'Also, if you lot at the station are investigating negligence rather than a deliberate act of sabotage, you're not going to get very far, are you?'

'I'm not sure that's fair. Flint may have made up her mind, but that doesn't mean the rest of us have.'

'The rest of us? Meaning who?'

'Well, me... and... me, I suppose.'

Liz gave him a triumphant look. 'Exactly. You need my help.'

Kevin didn't contradict her.

'Motive is the key. The obvious one is money. I imagine Grogan was quite well off?'

Kevin nodded. 'He's a jeweller. He owns Grogan's Gems on Baxtergate, but most of his business was done online. He has a big house at Sandsend, which suggests he made a pretty decent living.'

'Who gets it all now?' asked Liz.

'The usual, I suppose. His family. His wife.'

'Do you know how long he and Carolyn have been married?'

'Only a few months, apparently.'

'Interesting.'

'Reading between the lines, I don't think the rest of his family is happy about it. He has two sons, Philip and Adam, and a daughter, Helen, from his first wife... I can't remember her name.'

'Deborah,' said Liz. 'She plays piano for the choir. They got divorced last year. I wonder whether he and Carolyn were having an affair before that.'

'*Hell hath no fury?*'

'Maybe. But if Carolyn inherits everything, that wouldn't be ideal, would it? From Deborah's point of view?'

'Hardly. I'll see if I can get a copy of the will, if there is one. I'll have to be careful, though. Flint's made up her mind and won't be happy if she thinks I'm investigating a different theory. She won't want to upset the Grogans.'

'I suppose we'll be needing a new mayor now,' said Liz.

'I hadn't thought of that... but, yes, I suppose so.'

'Might be worth looking at whoever's next in line?'

'I should think it's democratic. And anyway, surely someone wouldn't kill him for that?'

'Politics is a murky business.'

'You've been watching too much TV.' Kevin grinned. 'This is Whitby, not *The West Wing*.' He looked at his watch. 'Better go. No point winding Flint up for no reason.'

Liz unhooked the green evening bag from the back of her chair. 'Can you take this with you? Put it in lost property? Someone left it behind at the party.' She didn't think there was any need to muddy the waters by mentioning that Mags and Tilly had picked it up accidentally. She had called the taxi company that morning, only to be told they'd taken dozens of people to the museum. If the writing hadn't been so smudged, they might have been able to guess who the bag belonged to from the driver and the fare, but as it was, there was no way of knowing.

Kevin took the bag from Liz. 'Nice shade of green. A bit like Anna's eyes.'

Liz gave him an amused look. To her astonishment, he blushed and shuffled awkwardly.

'With everything else that was going on the other night,' he said, 'I didn't get the chance to ask you what you thought of her.'

'She seems lovely. Shy, but lovely.' Liz smiled at him. 'I take it you're pretty serious, then?'

'I am.'

When Kevin had gone, Liz took her laptop out to do some research. She found the company information on Grogan's Gems. There were three names listed on the board of directors – Neil Grogan, Philip Grogan... and Walter Duguid. Liz had crossed paths with Wally Duguid in the summer. He had been less than honest in his business dealings. He was dead now, but his association with Neil Grogan made her think that maybe the mayor wasn't quite as squeaky clean as everyone imagined.

WITH LESS THAN two weeks to go before Christmas, the narrow streets of the old town were crowded, and the more modern ones on the other side of the harbour were even busier. It felt slightly warmer than it had been, and the herring gulls were back to their usual raucous selves, squabbling over scraps on the pavements. There were signs on the quayside warning people not to feed the gulls, but that didn't stop visitors from sneaking them food. The huge, sleek birds were a nuisance, and locals tried to discourage them.

Baxtergate was one of the main shopping streets of the town. It was quite a narrow Victorian thoroughfare, with banks, estate agents, and many of the chain stores you would expect to find on an English high street. There were a few independent shops sprinkled among them. Grogan's Gems had an impressive double frontage, with glossy black paintwork and gold signage. Liz had been past it many times, but had never been inside. Jewellery wasn't really her thing, and even if it were, she would have been discouraged by the shop's high-end appearance. The windows were impressive, with velvet displays and artful lighting. There were a few modern pieces showcased there – a dozen or so diamond engagement rings – but it was mostly antique jewellery:

heavy gold Albert chains, rings with emerald cut and old mine cut gems, charm bracelets and dress earrings. There were a few Georgian pieces too – black enamelled mourning rings, and beautiful paste drop earrings. Liz admired their beauty, but wouldn't want the responsibility of owning them.

She took a deep breath. If she wanted to find out more about the Grogan family, this was a good place to start. She had thought about asking Tilly to come with her, but had decided against it. Tilly was supposed to be rehabilitated, but Liz didn't want to push her too far. Taking her into Grogan's Gems would be like taking a toddler into a sweetshop and then forbidding them to eat anything. Liz squared her shoulders and walked in.

The bell gave a discreet 'bing-bong', and her feet sank into thick carpet. Too late, she realised she hadn't wiped her boots on the doormat, and was leaving wet footprints behind her. She smothered the urge to turn and run, and approached the glass display counter. As she did, someone emerged from the door behind it – a tall man with a very neat goatee, dressed in a white shirt and a waistcoat with a Victorian fob chain across the front. He was somewhere in his late thirties. Liz guessed it was probably Philip, the eldest son. Liz gave him a smile. He returned it with one that failed to reach his eyes.

'Can I help you?'

Liz felt his gaze as it travelled over her, taking in her puffa jacket, fingerless mittens and salt-stained walking boots. She resisted the urge to tuck her curls more neatly into her woollen hat.

'Yes, I'm looking for a present.'

Philip Grogan raised his eyebrows.

'For my sister.' Liz's sister, Julie, was currently trekking somewhere in India, and wouldn't be caught dead wearing expensive jewellery, but Philip Grogan wasn't to know that.

'What sort of thing do you have in mind?'

Liz shrugged. 'A pair of earrings? She has pierced ears.'

'Yellow gold? White gold? Rose gold? Platinum? Diamond? Pearl? Emerald? Opal?'

Is he trying to bludgeon me with possibilities?

'Yellow gold,' she said. 'Something discreet.'

He went to fetch a tray from one of the cabinets behind her. It had rows of beautiful earrings in many different styles. She touched one gently with the tip of her finger.

'Those are Edwardian Dormeuse earrings,' he said. 'French.'

'They're lovely.' Liz couldn't help but notice that none of the pieces had prices on. 'But I'm not sure they're really her style.' Another tray in the display case she was leaning on caught her eye. A selection of stick pins. 'Oh, what's that?'

It was a gold leaping hare with a small red stone for an eye. Julie loved hares. Philip took the tray out of the case and handed her the pin.

'Hallmarked Birmingham, eighteen eighty-five. The eye is a Burmese ruby.' He was watching her closely. 'It's five hundred and ninety pounds.'

She couldn't prevent a little squeak of dismay.

'There are some jewellery shops... chain stores... in Flowergate. You might find something there.'

Liz felt a flash of anger and retaliated.

'I was sorry to hear about your father,' she said.

'Pardon me?' Philip stiffened, and something flickered over his face. It happened very, very quickly, but Liz caught it. She didn't think it was grief.

'Your father. He was a very good mayor. The town will miss him.'

'If you say so.' Not the response you would expect from a grieving son. Philip's lip had curled. He couldn't seem to help it.

Liz pressed further. 'He owned this shop, didn't he?' She knew she was pushing her luck and being horribly rude, but her hackles were up. 'What will happen to it now?'

Philip leaned down to return the hare to the display case. When he stood up again, his face was carefully neutral.

'Is there anything else I can show you, madam?'

Liz couldn't really blame him for not answering her questions. She'd been very rude.

'I don't think so, thank you. You've been very helpful.'

And so he had. As Liz made her way out of the shop and back onto the pavement, she could feel his eyes on her.

She headed thoughtfully back to the East Cliff. What she'd seen on Philip Grogan's face when she'd mentioned his father wasn't love or grief or pain. It was resentment. There clearly wasn't much love lost between them. If Carolyn now inherited everything, Philip was potentially out of a job. If not – if Neil had made provision for Philip in his will – the status quo regarding the business would likely stay the same. Which was problematic. Either way, Philip Grogan wasn't likely to benefit from his father's death. If anything, he could be worse off. It was hardly a motive for murder.

5

'I'm sorry, but we won't be able to get anyone to look at it until after the New Year.'

'I have spare roof tiles. It should be quite a quick job.'

'I'm afraid that doesn't really make a difference. It's almost Christmas, and we're fully booked. You're more than welcome to try another roofer, Mrs McLuckie, but I doubt you'll be able to find anyone who can do it sooner.'

'Of course. Well, just fit me in as soon as you can, please, and I'll keep my fingers crossed we don't get any bad weather.'

When she'd hung up, Liz sighed. That wasn't great news, but there wasn't much she could do about it. Luckily, the weather forecast wasn't too bad – not too wet or windy. Whitby didn't often get snow, as the salt air tended to melt anything before it got the chance to lie. There could be snow-drifts shoulder high on the moors just a couple of miles away, but nothing at all on the ground in Whitby itself. She just hoped the forecast was accurate, and the weather behaved itself until the missing tiles could be replaced.

Liz looked around her kitchen. It was rather cheerless, with not a piece of tinsel nor bauble in sight. It made her wonder – why was she depriving herself of Christmas joy? She'd told herself she couldn't bear to put up decorations on her own, but wasn't that a bit pathetic? Was she really such a martyr? She blinked back a tear.

'Come on, Nelson,' she said. 'Let's get ourselves a tree.'

There was a pop-up Christmas tree shop on Tin Ghaut car park, at the quayside. Liz reckoned that as long as she didn't buy a huge tree, it should be quite easy to drag back to Henrietta Street. The sign at the entrance said 'Christmas Trees for sale – sizes to suit all'. The plot was large, stacked with trees, and at the far end there was a netting machine and a hut. She thought about taking Nelson in with her, but had a fleeting vision of him lifting his leg against one of the trees, and decided not to. She took her mittens off, tied Nelson to the sign, and went in on her own.

It didn't take her long to realise the sign had lied. There were plenty of trees, but they were all too big. She supposed that most people had their trees up by now, and the predominance of small cottages in the town had meant the smaller trees had gone first. She had just resigned herself to trying somewhere else when she spotted a tree in the middle of the row. It had a lovely bushy shape and only came to shoulder height. Perfect! She hurried to get it.

She pulled it, but it wouldn't budge. It took her a moment to realise there was someone holding onto it from the other side. She peered through the branches and saw a face with red cheeks, topped with an old-fashioned cloche hat – Dora Spackle, curator of the abbey museum. Liz was glad Nelson was safely tied up on the other side of the plot. Dora and Nelson hated each other with a passion, thanks to an incident the Christmas before involving a chewed handbag and a kick that had – thankfully – missed Nelson by a whisker.

Dora glowered at Liz through the branches. 'This is my tree,' she hissed. 'Get your own.'

'I don't think so,' countered Liz. 'I saw it first.' She had no idea if that was true, but now she had her hands on the tree, she wasn't going to let it go. Not for Dora Spackle.

Dora tugged the tree towards her. 'You did not.'

Liz tugged it back.

'GIVE IT TO ME,' yelled Dora. She gave an almighty heave that unbalanced Liz and made her topple forward. She landed hard. Luckily she had her puffa jacket on, and that had cushioned her fall, but she'd scraped her palms painfully on the gravel. Dora looked down at her with a smirk of satisfaction.

YIP, YIP!

Dora's smirk fled.

YIP, YIP! Nelson charged round the end of the line of trees like cavalry. Even though he was tied to the sign, it hadn't prevented him from coming to Liz's rescue when he heard Dora's raised voice. The sign was still attached to the end of his lead and clattered along dangerously behind him.

'Keep him off me!' shrieked Dora.

He bounded up to her, dragging the sign with him. Dora tried to ward him off with the tree, but it was too heavy to wield successfully. After a moment or two of unsuccessful poking and prodding, she gave up, abandoned the tree and made a run for it.

Nelson ran after her, snarling and yipping. Liz, who was still lying on the ground, made a grab for his trailing lead as the sign bounced past her. She had it briefly in her grasp, but Nelson was too strong, and it pulled through her fingers. She scrambled painfully to her feet.

Nelson caught up with Dora at the entrance. Liz closed her eyes as she hurried towards them.

'Please God, don't bite her,' she prayed. She opened

one eye.

Nelson had Dora at bay, snarling and snapping around her ankles.

Just as Liz reached them, Dora got her feet tangled in the lead and tumbled backwards. She landed hard on her backside, her teeth snapping together with a savage CLICK.

Liz managed to grab the lead, and hauled Nelson away. She looked around to see if they had an audience. There was no one in sight, but the tree had gone. While they'd been fighting, someone else had quietly taken it. She supposed it served them both right.

'Are you okay?' Liz held out her hand to Dora. Dora clearly thought about refusing it, but needed the help. She allowed Liz to pull her to her feet, winced and rubbed her backside.

'I can barely walk now.' She stabbed a finger at Liz. 'That dog of yours is a menace.'

'I'm sorry.' Nelson was now standing perfectly well behaved, ignoring Dora. He knew he'd beaten her.

Dora knew it too. 'I'm going to the police station.'

Liz looked at her in dismay. 'You're bleeding.' There was a trickle of blood on Dora's chin. Dora wiped it away with her fingers and stared at the blood.

'I've cut my lip,' she muttered. Tears sprang into her eyes.

Liz took pity on her. 'You can't go to the station like that. Let's get you cleaned up.'

The Captain Cook Maritime Museum on Grape Lane was only a minute's walk away, but it was still a struggle to get there, with Dora leaning heavily on one of Liz's arms, and Nelson pulling at the other. The museum was a tall, narrow eighteenth-century building that backed onto the quayside. Inside, it was a warren of crooked rooms and passageways, criss-crossed with beams, full of displays of sailing ships, knots and other seafaring memorabilia. Benedict spotted them through the internal window of his office as they staggered in.

'What happened?' he asked, clearly alarmed by their dishevelment and Dora's bloody chin.

'What do you think?' said Liz, glaring at Nelson.

Benedict's eyes slid to the bull terrier, who looked nonchalantly at the ceiling.

Benedict grimaced. 'Let me take him.' He took the lead from Liz. 'There's a first aid box in the ladies' loo.'

Liz steered Dora in there. Dora examined her lip in the mirror while Liz pulled a paper towel from the dispenser and ran it under the tap. 'Here,' she said, 'clean the blood off, and I'll look for the first aid kit.'

She found it in the cupboard and rummaged through it until she found some antiseptic cream. She gave it to Dora and watched as she dabbed some on her freshly cleaned lip.

'That doesn't look too bad,' said Liz.

'I'm still going to the police,' sniffed Dora.

Liz sighed. 'That's up to you.'

'That friend of yours from the café might be there too if they've arrested her. She killed the mayor with her terrible food.'

'That's not true.' It was a vicious attack, even for Dora.

'Of course it is. I was there. The meat in her sausage rolls was raw. I went into the kitchen to tell her so, but she wasn't there, so I showed Adam Grogan. He agreed with me. It was completely raw.'

Liz seriously doubted that. Dora was just being spiteful. But then a thought occurred.

'Adam Grogan was in the kitchen?'

Dora looked blankly at Liz.

'What was he doing there?'

'Same as me, probably. Complaining about the food. Or trying to.' Dora sniffed and fastened her coat. 'Now, I'm going to the police to report that dog of yours. And you can't stop me.'

Liz held up her hands in surrender.

Dora stomped out.

Liz tossed Dora's bloody paper towel in the bin and ran her stinging palms under the tap. She caught her reflection in the mirror and looked away. She couldn't quite believe she'd stooped so low as to brawl with Dora.

There was a knock at the door. 'All okay?' Benedict stuck his head in. 'She's gone. Are you hurt?'

'My hands.'

He joined her. 'Let me see.' She gave him her hands, and he peered at her palms. 'Ouch. Looks like you've got some gravel in there. Let's take the first aid kit through to my office. I have some tweezers.'

She followed him into his office, where Nelson was blissfully asleep on the rug beside the electric fire. Benedict made her sit on his chair. Suddenly she felt very warm and took her hat off.

'I'm sure they're in here somewhere,' he said, looking in his desk drawers. 'I used them the other day to fix the rigging on one of the models. Here we go!' He looked at the tweezers doubtfully. 'Maybe I should sterilise them first?'

'The antiseptic will be enough,' she said. 'Just get it over with.'

He raised an eyebrow. 'Okay, scaredy-cat.'

He'd misunderstood. It wasn't the prospect of pain that was making her nervous, but of being so close to him.

'Lift your hands up,' he said, 'so I can see them properly.'

She lifted her palms to the light, and he examined them. 'It's only a few bits, but it is going to sting getting them out.' He took one of her hands gently and bent over it. He was so close she could feel his body heat radiating off him, and smell his aftershave.

'Here we go.' She could feel his breath on her hand. And then a stinging pain.

'Ow!' She pulled her hand away.

'You have to stay still.' He frowned at her. She'd never been so close to him before. She could see his grey irises were flecked with amber.

'Okay,' she muttered. 'Sorry.'

He bent over her hand again. 'I'll do it as gently as I can.'

She kept very still as, one by one, he extracted half a dozen pieces of grit and put them carefully on the desk.

'Now the other one.'

She gave him her other hand and steeled herself not to flinch as the tweezers jabbed into her palm. It took longer than she expected.

'Okay. I think that's it. Well done.' He was still holding her hand. Their eyes locked and held. Something flickered on Benedict's face. Liz held her breath. Her heart thumped.

GRRRR!

Nelson was on his feet, scowling at Benedict.

Benedict released Liz's hand. 'He thinks I'm hurting you.'

'You are.'

Benedict flashed her an uncertain look, then passed her the tube of antiseptic cream. He turned to Nelson. 'What's up with you, old man? I thought we were friends.'

Nelson padded over to Benedict and allowed him to rub his ears while Liz put cream on her palms. When she'd finished, Benedict took the tube from her and replaced it in the first aid kit. Whatever she'd seen on his face – or thought she'd seen – was gone.

'Better put this back where it belongs,' he said, and went out with the first aid kit.

Liz glared at Nelson.

'Man's best friend, my backside,' she muttered.

6

'A little bird tells me you're friends with Mrs Gladwell?'

'Erm... yes?' Liz could guess what was coming next.

'I was wondering' – Gregory Willis hesitated on the phone – 'whether you might have a word with her before choir practice. Ask her if she can turn down the volume a little.'

'I'm not really sure she can,' said Liz. 'Iris has really only ever had one volume – deafening. It doesn't make any difference whether she's talking or singing.'

'Oh.'

Liz could sense his desperation. 'But I'll have a word.'

'Would you? We've been asked to sing at the mayor's funeral as well as the carol service, but I'm not sure we can. Not with Mrs Gladwell and Crystal.'

'Deborah Grogan won't be at practice tonight, then?'

'I don't think we can count on her. She and her husband were married for many years, I believe.'

'I believe so.'

'I'll see you tonight, then... and thank you.'

Liz put the phone down and looked at Nelson, who had

been listening to the conversation. 'Poor man,' said Liz. 'He's clutching at straws.'

THE NEXT MORNING Liz called at Iris's cottage in Neptune Yard, but found it locked up tight and in darkness. It was only eight o'clock, but she knew that Iris was an early riser. At first Liz felt a pang of concern, but then realised the curtains were open. She knew the old lady always closed them at night. So where was she? The café was still technically closed, but Liz decided to call there anyway and take a look. It wasn't unusual for Tilly to let regulars in early. She made her way carefully back through the semi-darkness of the yard to the iron gate at the entrance.

There was no one else around. Most of the Christmas lights on Church Street were off, but the street lights were on. The sky was still black, with only the faintest lightening in the east that heralded dawn. Liz sighed. In these dark days it was all too easy to imagine the sun might never rise again.

As she approached the gothic Mission Chapel halfway down Church Street, she saw lights on inside. On impulse, she went up the steps and into the foyer, which was decorated with ornate Victorian tiles. The building had recently been converted by the council, and now was home to a restaurant and the Museum of Whitby Jet.

Whitby Jet was a fossilised gemstone found in the cliffs around Whitby. It was lightweight and easy to carve and polish, which made it perfect for jewellery. When Prince Albert died in 1861, Queen Victoria took to wearing Whitby Jet in remembrance of him. She thought so highly of it that it was the only jewellery allowed to be worn in court during her protracted mourning period.

The main body of the chapel was now the restaurant, and the warren of rooms in front of it housed the museum. It had a modern glass facade, which served as the entrance and shop. Liz spotted Deborah Grogan inside and tapped on the glass.

Deborah jumped and peered to see who had knocked. She hurried to open the door.

'You gave me quite a fright there, Liz.'

'Sorry. I saw the lights on.' Liz hesitated. 'I thought I'd come and offer my condolences.'

A shadow passed over Deborah's face. 'It's very kind of you to think of me.' There was a definite trace of bitterness in her voice. 'You're almost the only person who has.'

'It must be very hard.'

Deborah pulled a regretful face. She was tall, with strong, good-natured features, the sort of woman Liz's mother liked to call handsome. She was always very well put together. Today she was wearing a dark grey cashmere sweater with a cowl neck, and a discreet pair of Jet earrings dangling at her ears.

'I was just putting some new stock in the shop,' she said. 'Why not come in and keep me company?'

Liz hesitated.

'Please? I've been horribly on edge the last few days. Silly, really.'

Liz didn't think it was silly at all. She followed Deborah into the shop and watched as she unpacked a box of cellophane-wrapped jewellery.

'It must have been a terrible shock.'

Deborah sighed. 'There was always a possibility it would happen someday. I used to carry an EpiPen with me everywhere, even when the kids were little. Philip accidentally jabbed himself once, with one he found in my pocket.'

'Oh no! Was he okay?'

'Luckily he didn't get the full dose. But after that I was very careful to keep it zipped up when we were out and about.' Deborah hooked several pairs of silver and Jet earrings through the display tree on the counter. The jewellery for sale in the shop was all modern, and although it was nice enough, Liz thought it looked rather flimsy compared to the artfully lit pieces in the display cases in the back section that led through to the museum. Liz wandered over to look in one of them.

The centrepiece was a gorgeous snake bangle, heavily carved and coiled. It was flanked by several intricately carved cameo brooches.

'Beautiful, aren't they?' said Deborah over her shoulder. 'Would you like a proper look?'

Liz nodded. She'd never actually been in the museum itself. Deborah reached through the archway and flicked on a bank of switches. All the display cases lit up inside. Each small room led into another and then another, each one lined with display cases. Some of the larger rooms also had free-standing cabinets. Liz and Deborah wandered through the rooms together, looking at the jewellery.

'Where does it all come from?'

'Some is on loan from other museums, and some has been donated from private collections. There's still a surprising amount of it about. People used to bring them in to the shop. Neil liked to buy it whenever he could, for as little as he could.'

That didn't surprise Liz. Wally Duguid had been a director of the company, so it made sense that Neil Grogan had similar ethics. But what about Deborah?

'You didn't agree with that?' pressed Liz.

'Of course not! A lot of it was estate. It was wrong to take advantage of people who were grieving. I much prefer it here in the museum, where I can enjoy these beautiful pieces without having to deal with the grubby commercial side of things.' She pointed at one of the cases. 'This is one of my favourites.'

Nestled among some other sea-themed pieces was an impressively heavy-looking brooch – an anchor with a trailing chain, each link threaded with a carved rope.

'I don't know why,' said Deborah, 'but I've always had an affinity for the stuff. It's funny, isn't it? That something so ordinary – wood – can be transformed by nature into something with such potential for beauty? Beauty that needs a human hand to unlock it. Man and Mother Nature in harmony.'

Which reminded Liz.

'It's choir practice tonight,' she said. 'I don't suppose you're coming?'

Deborah looked doubtful.

Liz pressed. 'Crystal's lovely, but... she is quite rusty. We've been asked to sing at Neil's funeral, but I've heard Gregory's thinking about turning it down.'

'Really?' Deborah looked concerned. 'That would be a shame.'

'It would.' Liz didn't say that Gregory's desperation wasn't just because of Crystal's piano playing. In her experience, full disclosure wasn't always the best course of action.

'I might come,' said Deborah. 'I'll see how I feel. But now I should get back to work.'

WHEN SHE LEFT THE MUSEUM, Liz went to the café, but Iris wasn't there. In fact, no one was. The café was locked up and in darkness. A sign on the door just said 'Closed Today' with no explanation.

Liz dialled Tilly's number. It went straight to answerphone.

What was going on?

It wasn't until later that afternoon that Liz eventually managed to speak to Tilly. She was inspecting the ceiling of her attic bedroom, trying to see if the hole in the roof was visible from inside. Apart from a small damp patch on the plaster, there was no obvious sign of it. Her phone rang. She fumbled to answer it.

'Tilly! Are you okay?'

'*We're fine.*' But her voice was weary. '*Sorry, I should have called you back before now.*'

'What's going on?'

'*We got a letter this morning from Carolyn Grogan's solicitor. She's definitely going to sue for negligence. Mags has gone back to bed, and I just didn't have the heart to open up this morning.*'

'Are you going to fight it?'

'*We'll try, but it's hard. The police know that Mags fried the tempura in sesame oil, and Carolyn told us about the mayor's sesame allergy in an email. She can prove it.*'

'But someone swapped the oil.'

'*We can't prove that. There's only Mags's word she made a special oil in the first place.*' The tone of Tilly's voice brought Liz up short.

'You do believe her, don't you?'

'*Of course.*' But it lacked conviction.

'Look, the oil that Mags made can't have just disappeared. Is there any sign of it in the café?'

'*No.*'

'Well, that's good, isn't it? It shows that Mags didn't just mistakenly bring sesame oil instead. The oil she took to the museum was the one she made.'

'*I suppose.*'

'Come on, Tilly. Don't give up. Fight for your lady. We'll get to the bottom of this, I promise.'

. . .

MY SOUL GIVE praise unto the Lord of Heaven
MY SOUL GIVE PRAISE UNTO THE LORD OF HEAVEN!
In Majesty and honour clothed.
IN MAJESTY AND HONOUR CLOTHED!
Iris bludgeoned her way through Psalm 104 like a cannon-ball. When they'd finished, the rest of the Eskside Singers sneaked horrified glances at each other.

'Okay, everyone.' Gregory sighed. 'Let's break there.' He looked accusingly at Liz, who pulled an apologetic face. She hadn't had the chance to speak to Iris before choir practice.

She finally caught up with her by the refreshment table, where she was talking to Benedict.

'Where were you this morning?' Liz asked her. 'I was looking for you.'

'IRWIN TOOK ME TO YORK TO DO SOME CHRISTMAS SHOPPING.' Iris eyed the plate of assorted biscuits with suspicion. 'IS THAT JAM IN THEM BISCUITS? I CAN'T BE ON WITH IT TODAY.' She had arcane and unfathomable rules about jam and when she could eat it.

Deborah joined them. Her expression was stiff – she was clearly regretting giving in to Liz's entreaty to come. She forced a smile.

'Lovely to have new members,' she said to Iris. 'Will you be joining us permanently, Mrs Gladwell?'

'OH, I SHOULD THINK SO.' Iris pushed a chocolate biscuit into her mouth and spoke around it. 'I'M REALLY ENJOYING MYSELF.'

Across the room, Liz could see that Gregory had button-holed Irwin. From the look on their faces, they were having a very earnest discussion. As Liz watched them, someone else appeared in the doorway – a slight figure with elfin features, wearing jeans and a clerical collar. The Reverend Gillian Garraway hesitated, her gaze scanning the room. Benedict stiffened as their eyes met. She came towards them.

'Liz, Benedict, can I have a word, please?' She led them into a quiet corner, away from the others.

'Sorry for bothering you both,' said Gillian. 'I hope you don't mind?'

'Of course not,' said Benedict. But Liz knew that he *did* mind, because the left-hand corner of his mouth had just twitched. The tell was almost imperceptible, but infallible. Liz had first noticed it during their regular mah-jong nights in the summer, but even though she'd warned Benedict, he couldn't seem to do anything about it.

'I didn't know who else to turn to,' continued Gillian. 'I don't want to get the police involved unless I have to, and you're the cleverest people I know.' She took a deep breath. 'Neil Grogan's missing.'

'What?' said Liz.

Benedict frowned. 'But he's...'

'Dead.' Gillian nodded. 'Yes, I know. Until about an hour ago he was lying in my church, dead as a doornail. But now he's gone.'

7

St Mary's church, perched on the East Cliff high above the town, was squat and rather unprepossessing. Originally founded in the twelfth century, it had been rebuilt several times, and its exterior gave no hint to the gothic delights within. The eighteenth-century interior had box pews, a three-tier pulpit, and a transept supported by white barley-twist columns, bejewelled in daylight hours with light from stained-glass windows.

Now, however, the windows were dark, and the church's aisles were gloomy. Neil Grogan's coffin stood slightly askew on trestles in the nave, its lid off, and its padded interior empty. Liz and Benedict stared at it.

'The Grogans are coming,' said Gillian. 'They'll be here any minute. What am I going to tell them?'

'Isn't it unusual to have an overnight vigil these days?' asked Liz.

Gillian nodded. 'I don't think the family were keen, but he'd always said he wanted a church vigil the night before his funeral. Why would someone do this?'

'I don't suppose the funeral parlour might have taken him away again for some reason?' suggested Liz.

'Without telling me? Without his coffin? I shouldn't think so.'

It was baffling.

Benedict inspected the stone flags around the trestles.

'What are you looking for?' asked Gillian.

'You can't move a man like Neil Grogan without some kind of effort. Without leaving a trace.' Benedict knelt to inspect a small patch of mud. 'I take it you still don't have CCTV in here?'

''Fraid not,' said Gillian.

Liz was surprised. She had imagined that the shocking events of the summer, when a murder was actually committed in the church, might have prompted the committee to install them. She sniffed the air.

'Is it my imagination,' she said, 'or is there an odd smell in here?'

Benedict and Gillian both sniffed too.

'I can't smell anything,' said Benedict. 'But I'm getting a cold. Probably caught it off Mags.'

'There is something,' insisted Liz. 'Something sweet.'

'The flowers?' suggested Gillian. There were several displays of lilies dotted around the church.

'Or maybe it was the body,' said Benedict. 'Embalming fluid?'

'Maybe,' said Liz. She didn't think it was the lilies. It did smell familiar, though, and as far as she knew, she'd never smelled embalming fluid before. Benedict gave up his inspection of the floor.

'How did they get in?' he asked.

'Through the door. It wasn't locked. I took ill quite suddenly.' Gillian blushed. 'I had to go to the bathroom.'

'Had you eaten anything?' asked Liz.

'Only my coffee. I bring it in a flask, to keep me awake through the night.'

'Can I take a look?'

Gillian disappeared into the vestry and reappeared holding a stainless-steel vacuum flask. Liz took it and sniffed the liquid inside.

'Do you think someone put something in it?' asked Gillian.

'Hard to tell,' said Liz. 'It just smells of coffee.'

'I did take ill very suddenly.'

Liz rescrewed the lid on the flask.

'I'm sorry for bothering you both with this,' said Gillian. 'I'm not entirely sure why I did, really.'

'Because we're your friends,' said Liz firmly. 'I know we haven't seen much of you lately, but we are.'

Gillian's eyes flashed to Benedict. 'Really?'

Benedict nodded, but didn't hold her gaze.

Liz felt awkward. She knew exactly why Gillian had broken off with Benedict, and it wasn't his fault, but Gillian had sworn her to secrecy. It had put Liz in a difficult position, especially in the early days after the break-up when she could see how much Benedict was hurting. But lately he had seemed to be getting over it. She remembered, with a sudden flush of warmth, the moment that had passed between them in the museum. Had she just imagined it?

'You have to phone the police,' said Benedict to Gillian. His tone was businesslike. 'It will look bad if you haven't done anything by the time the family get here.'

Gillian looked crestfallen, but nodded.

'Would you like me to call Kevin?' asked Benedict in a slightly gentler tone.

'If you don't mind. Thank you.'

He took out his mobile and frowned. 'I can't get a signal in here. I'll take it outside.'

When he'd gone, Liz and Gillian sat down together on the front pew. They stared at the empty coffin for a few minutes.

'How is he?' asked Gillian.

It took a moment for Liz to realise she was talking about Benedict and not their missing mayor. 'Better, I think.'

'Good. I shouldn't have come to you. I don't know what I was thinking.'

'Don't be daft. You did the right thing.' Liz hesitated. She knew she had to say something more, even if it wasn't in her own best interests. 'You know it's not too late.'

'What?'

'To pick things up again with Benedict. To explain.'

Gillian shook her head. 'That's all water under the bridge. Honestly. It's kinder now to *everyone* just to let it go.' The emphasis had been on '*everyone*'. Their eyes locked together.

'What do you bloody mean, he's gone?' Philip Grogan stomped into the church and strode up the aisle. He was followed closely by Benedict and three other figures. Liz recognised Carolyn, dressed warmly for her vigil in a black padded jacket and trousers. The man behind her was about the same age, attractive in a ruddy-cheeked, rugby-playing kind of way. The young woman who trailed after them had a long, pale face and was dressed in grey jeans and hooded jacket. Liz guessed they were Grogan's younger son, Adam, and his daughter, Helen. She thought that Helen was married, but if so, her husband wasn't with her.

Philip arrived at the coffin and looked inside.

'What the hell?'

Carolyn hurried to join him at the coffin. 'Where is he?' she asked Gillian. 'What have you done with him?'

'Nothing. I went to the bathroom, and when I came out, he was gone.'

Carolyn glared at her. 'You left him here on his own?'

'To be fair,' snapped Gillian, 'I wasn't expecting him to

wander off.' She back-pedalled. 'I'm sorry. I have no idea where he went.'

'What are we going to do?' asked Helen. Her nose was red. From crying, Liz supposed.

'We'll have to call the police,' said Adam.

'I've done that,' said Benedict. 'They're on the way.'

'This is horrible!' Carolyn covered her face. 'Just horrible.' Adam tentatively put his arm around her.

'I don't understand,' said Philip. 'It makes no sense. Who on earth would steal a body?'

No one had an answer to that. They all looked at each other awkwardly.

Carolyn shrugged off Adam's arm and blew her nose. Her gaze alighted on Liz.

'I know you. You were at the café.'

'You were in the shop, too.' Philip's eyes narrowed suspiciously. 'What are you doing here?'

'She's my friend,' said Gillian.

'That doesn't really answer the question though, does it?' said Philip. He looked at Benedict. 'And who are you?'

'Commander Benedict Ossett.' He didn't often use his naval title. He drew himself up to his full height. 'I'm a friend of Gillian... Reverend Garraway... too.'

Gillian threw him a grateful look.

Philip looked suspiciously at Liz and Benedict. 'What is this? A sightseeing tour? What are you both doing here?'

'A very good question.' Someone else had entered the church and now stood dramatically in the aisle. Detective Inspector Fiona Flint, dressed in an immaculate skirt suit and trainers, put her hands on her hips and glared at them. As usual, Liz marvelled at how well groomed she was. There was no sign of grey in her expertly coloured and bobbed hair, even though Liz was pretty sure she was in her late forties. Kevin stood behind Flint, accompanied by the slouching figure of DC Williams. Williams had a long, mournful face, more suited to a Victorian undertaker than a policeman.

Flint advanced down the aisle towards the little group, with a long-legged stride. She looked at the empty coffin, and her eyebrows rose.

'What's going on?'

'As I said on the phone,' began Benedict, 'the reverend was taken ill, and—'

'Not you, Mr Ossett.' Flint's emphasis on the Mr was subtle but insulting. 'I prefer my information from the horse's mouth.' She turned to Gillian. 'Reverend?'

Gillian took a deep breath. 'The funeral parlour delivered Mr Grogan and set up the coffin. About half an hour later I had to go to the bathroom. When I came out, he was gone.'

Flint's eyebrows rose even further. 'Why would—' She broke off. 'Williams, shouldn't you be taking notes?'

DC Williams's long, lugubrious face grew even longer as he fumbled for his notebook. Flint turned back to the group. She spotted Carolyn. 'I'm sorry for your loss, Mrs Grogan. Everyone in the force thought very highly of your husband.' She shook Carolyn's hand. 'You have my personal assurance we will find him.'

Liz realised that Flint was enjoying herself. It was hard to watch. She started to sidle away.

Flint's head snapped round. 'Where are you going?'

'I... um... I really shouldn't be here. I'm just getting in the way.'

'You'll go when I say you can go. Why is it that whenever something happens in this town, I always find you right in the middle of it? What are you doing here?'

'Sorry,' DC Williams interrupted. 'Excuse me, but does anyone have a pen?'

Flint glared at him in disbelief.

'I can't find mine,' he muttered.

'I think I have one in my bag,' volunteered Helen. She opened her bag to look.

'It's okay,' said Kevin. 'Here you go.' He gave Williams a pen from his pocket.

'Thanks.'

Flint shot Williams a withering glare, then turned back to Liz. 'You haven't answered my question, Mrs McLuckie. Why are you here?'

'The reverend came to me and Commander Ossett for help when she realised Mr Grogan was missing.'

Flint's gaze snapped to Gillian. 'Rather than call the police? You seem to have your priorities wrong.' She raked them all with her gaze, but it came to rest on Liz. 'Let me be totally clear. I will find Mr Grogan's body, without amateur interference.'

Liz noted the 'I' rather than 'we'. She caught DC Williams's eye. From the way his lips twitched, she could tell he'd also noted the pronoun.

'First things first,' snapped Flint. 'Let's get the timeline straight. Then we can go from there. Reverend, come and sit down over here, please. Ossett, take notes. Do you have a pen, or do you need the North Yorkshire Police Force pen back from Williams?'

Kevin clearly thought it was best to ignore her sarcasm. He went to join her and Gillian. The Grogans stood in a huddle near the coffin. DC Williams joined Liz and Benedict.

'Commander, Mrs Mac.' He acknowledged them both with a nod.

'Detective Constable.' If he'd been out of uniform, Liz would have called him Bill.

'This is a bit weird, eh?'

'Just a bit,' agreed Liz.

Williams's nose twitched. 'What's that funny smell?'

'You can smell it too?' said Liz.

'Mmm. Kind of sweet. Like medicine.'

Benedict blew his nose, then sniffed. 'Sorry. I still can't smell it. It's probably from the corpse. They use lots of stuff to mask the smell.'

'Keep your voice down,' Liz whispered. She saw that Helen Grogan's pale, anxious face was turned towards them, and felt a wave of sympathy. It was bad enough that Helen's father should have died so suddenly, without his body going missing too.

DC Williams's thoughts moved on to practical matters. 'Whoever took the body had to have used a car. I might nip outside and take a look in the car park.'

'Can we come?' asked Benedict. 'We're not doing anything useful in here.'

'I don't see why not.' Williams glanced at Flint, who was deep in conversation with Gillian and Kevin. 'But please don't wander off. I'm supposed to be keeping an eye on you.'

Outside on the exposed clifftop, the wind was bitter, whipping through the long grass and whistling around ancient gravestones. Liz pulled her hat further over her ears. Williams took his regulation torch from his belt and shone it on the stone flags as they walked along the path that led to the walled car park, which served both the church and the museum. The car park only had three cars in it – Williams's squad car, the detectives' unmarked car, and a Range Rover the Grogans had arrived in. Liz and Benedict and DC Williams did a circuit of the car park together but saw nothing out of the ordinary apart from a tiny, rainbow-coloured sock that had probably fallen from a visitor's pushchair.

'It was worth a try.' Williams hung the sock on the museum gate, where it could be spotted by anyone who came looking for it.

'The council really should get CCTV up here,' said Benedict.

'They should,' agreed Williams.

A dark figure appeared at the entrance to the car park.

'What are you all doing out here?' shouted Kevin. 'Flint wants you.'

When they got back in the church, Flint made a beeline for them.

'I need a statement from you both.'

'I really don't think I can give you anything useful,' protested Liz.

'I'll be the judge of that.' Flint's eyes narrowed at her. 'I also need to have a word with you about your dog. We've had a complaint.'

'Dora,' said Liz.

'The case has been referred to the Council's Dangerous Dogs unit.'

'Dangerous? Nelson's not dangerous.'

'The complainant was injured.'

'Yes, but he didn't bite her. She just fell over him.'

'I can vouch for that,' chipped in Benedict. 'Dora wasn't bitten.'

Flint was unimpressed. 'It's still the responsibility of an owner to keep their animal under control. Was your dog under control?'

'Well, not exactly, but...'

'You'll be hearing from the council.' Flint turned to Benedict. 'Mr Ossett, I'll take your statement first.'

8

L iz watched Nelson as she ate her breakfast. He was sleeping in his basket, pink tummy exposed, tongue lolling, looking not in the least bit dangerous. She doubted she'd hear anything from the council before Christmas, but she supposed that depended on how much Dora had exaggerated the incident with the tree. She knew that the council had far-reaching powers when it came to dangerous dogs – they could take him away from her. They could even have him put down.

She blinked back tears. They would have to take him over her dead body.

She finished her breakfast, then took Gillian's flask from the kitchen counter. She stared at the cold coffee inside. Flint had refused to get it analysed, saying it didn't really matter whether it had been laced with anything. But Liz disagreed. If it had, it showed meticulous planning on the part of whoever had stolen Grogan's body, and, depending how quickly it took effect, it might give them a better indication of the timings involved. Liz hesitated, then swallowed a few mouthfuls.

Fifteen minutes later she had her answer. Her stomach

started to cramp painfully, and she only just made it upstairs to the bathroom. Over the next half an hour or so she couldn't do anything other than sit there and think. Who could possibly have stolen Neil Grogan's body, and why? From her interview in the church with Flint the evening before, it was clear the Detective Inspector didn't believe the theft had anything to do with his death. Flint still believed that Mags had caused his allergic reaction. But to Liz's mind, that was quite spectacularly short-sighted. Any one of the two occurrences – Grogan's death and his subsequent disappearance – was extraordinary. Taken together, they simply couldn't be a coincidence. The question was, did the same person who had deliberately swapped Mags's cooking oil also steal the body? If so, why? Could there have been something hidden in Grogan's body?

Liz thought about it. Grogan had just returned from a highly publicised trip to Cooktown, Australia, a town twinned with Whitby. Hadn't she read somewhere about Australia being a gateway for dodgy diamonds? Neil Grogan was a jeweller. Was there a connection there? If he'd swallowed diamonds to smuggle them into the country, and died before he was able to pass them, perhaps someone else was trying to retrieve them now? How long would they take to pass through his body?

From her own current situation, possibly not very long.

It was a twenty-four-hour trip back from Oz, without stopovers. How long had Grogan been back in the UK? If he'd had a stopover somewhere, could he have picked up his contraband there? Singapore? Hong Kong?

After playing with that idea for a few minutes, Liz dismissed it. It was too far-fetched. Then again, stealing a body was pretty far-fetched. Someone, somewhere must have had a good reason to do it. But what could it be?

She found herself going round in circles. It was a relief in more ways than one when she felt able to go downstairs again.

After taking Nelson for his belated morning walk, Liz passed a couple of hours wrapping presents. She never spent too much on Christmas gifts and always shopped in the town rather than online, to support local businesses. She'd bought some lovely hand-knitted socks and chocolates for Mags and Tilly, a bottle of vodka for Grazyna, Trivial Pursuit for the boys, shortbread for Iris and some Kendal mint cake for her young archaeologist friend, Niall Fitzgerald. After she'd wrapped Niall's present in wrapping paper, she put it in a padded envelope with his card and wrote his mum's Dublin address on it. Then she put on her coat.

'Come on, Nelson,' she said. 'Let's get some fresh air.'

The queue at the post office was out the door, so Liz and Nelson had to wait on the pavement. They hopped from foot to foot to keep warm. Luckily the queue was moving pretty quickly. They'd only been there a minute or two when the post office door opened, and a customer came out. Nelson's fur bristled, and he growled low in his throat. Dora Spackle gave them an ostentatiously wide berth, then pointed at the sign on the door that said NO DOGS. Liz ignored it. The postmistress knew Liz and Nelson and always made an exception. But Liz saw her chance and hurried after Dora.

'Dora, the police say...'

The museum curator just lifted her chin and stomped off. Liz wanted to shout something rude after her, but swallowed the impulse. She wouldn't help Nelson by antagonising Dora further. She rejoined the back of the queue.

After posting Niall's present, Liz took Nelson for a bracing walk along the pier. On the way home, Liz spotted a news stand. The headline of the *Whitby Bugle* blared 'Mayor Missing! Funeral postponed'. She went into the newsagents to buy a copy.

When she got back to Gull Cottage, she made herself some lunch and sat at the table to read the front page. It told her nothing she didn't already know apart from the fact that Grogan had been treasurer of the Whitby Philatelic Society and spokesperson for the North Yorkshire Association of Racehorse Owners. It seemed he'd been a man with a finger in many pies. There was also a quote in the article from Philip Grogan.

'It was bad enough my father dying so suddenly, thanks to someone's carelessness, but now to have his body stolen in such a bizarre manner is beyond belief. The police have assured us they will recover him as quickly as possible. In the meantime I would like to ask the citizens of Whitby to keep their eyes open, and if they hear anything unusual or suspicious regarding my missing father, to get in touch with Detective Inspector Flint.'

Liz wondered if Tilly and Mags had seen the paper. She knew the café was open again – she'd peered through the window as she and Nelson had passed earlier. There'd been no one inside except Grazyna, who had spotted her and raised a hand in weary salute. That worried Liz. The café was usually popular and should have been busy so close to Christmas. Was the Whitby rumour mill to blame? Had people heard about Mags's possible involvement in Grogan's death? Liz hoped not, but couldn't think of any other explanation for the Full Moon's sudden fall in popularity. She knew Mags would take it hard.

Her phone rang. It was Gregory Willis.

'We've moved our practice tonight to St Mary's. The acoustics are quite unusual in there. I want us to get used to them before the carol service.'

Liz was surprised. 'Isn't it supposed to be a crime scene?'

'*I've cleared it with the reverend. She says it's okay.*' He hesitated. '*I don't suppose you've managed to have a word with Mrs Gladwell?*'

'Sorry, no.'

He sighed. '*It's probably just as well the funeral was cancelled. It would have been a disaster. Let's hope we have time to sort things out before the carol service.*'

It was properly dark by four o'clock. After having something to eat and giving Nelson another, shorter walk along the shore, Liz got ready for choir practice. She decided to dress up a bit, in her red wool coat and a new pair of gloves she'd treated herself to – dark green leather with black faux-fur trim. She thought she looked very smart and Christmassy, although the overall effect was undermined a little by her salt-stained boots. Her boots had excellent rubber soles, great for gripping ice, and she told herself that safety was more important than style. She made sure she had a torch in her pocket, settled Nelson in his basket with one of his toys, and headed out.

When she got to the bottom of the abbey steps, she saw a figure coming out of Kiln Yard. It was Iris, bundled up like an Inuit.

'BLOODY BALTIC OUT HERE,' she bellowed, by way of greeting. 'GOOD JOB WE'RE NOT BRASS MONKEYS.'

'It is,' agreed Liz. 'Watch these steps. They're icy.' She offered Iris her arm, but the old woman flapped her away.

'I'M NOT THAT OLD. I DON'T NEED YOUR HELP.'

They went up the steps together. Even though the old-fashioned Victorian street lamps were on, they were haloed by frost and more decorative than useful. Liz lit their way up the treacherous steps with her torch, Iris huffing and puffing beside her.

'Isn't Irwin coming tonight?' asked Liz.

'HE HAD TO WORK. IT'S THAT TIME OF YEAR, ISN'T IT? PEOPLE DROPPING LIKE FLIES.'

Liz had no idea what Irwin did for a living. Perhaps he was a doctor? She was about to ask, but then realised this might be the perfect opportunity to broach the subject of Iris's singing.

'Iris—?'

'DID YOU HEAR ABOUT THE MAYOR?'

'Yes. I—'

'HE WAS ONE OF THEM MASONS, YOU KNOW. A TROUSER-HITCHER. THEY'VE PROBABLY TAKEN HIM OFF TO HAVE SOME KIND OF CEREMONY, LIKE IN *THE DA VINCI CODE*.'

'How do you know he was a Mason?'

Iris sniffed. 'EVERYONE KNOWS WHO THE TOWN MASONS ARE.'

Liz wasn't surprised. The Whitby community was friendly, but that had its drawbacks. It was almost impossible to keep a secret of any kind for very long. Liz thought it was interesting that Grogan had been a Freemason, but not particularly surprising, given his status. She doubted that had anything to do with his disappearance. As theories went, it was a long shot.

Liz heard a lot more theories when they got to the church. Everyone in the choir had a suggestion about what might have happened.

'Perhaps he was kidnapped?' suggested Crystal, the stand-in pianist, as she helped herself to tea from the urn. 'They might have sent a ransom note.'

'Maybe,' said someone else. 'A dead body is a lot less trouble than a live one. And Grogan was worth a few bob.'

'It isn't always about money,' said Robert Buckle, who owned a barber's shop on Flowergate. 'He's probably been stolen by organ thieves, who want to ship his bits to India.'

Benedict met Liz's eye and raised an eyebrow. Liz stifled a grin with her hand.

'THAT'S RUBBISH,' bellowed Iris. 'IT'S THEM RUDDY MASONS WHAT DID IT.'

'I heard he lost a lot of money on that horse of his,' said someone else. 'Those debt collectors can be nasty beggars. I bet he isn't dead at all. I bet he's on a plane to South America right now.'

'You look nice tonight,' said Benedict in Liz's ear. 'New coat?'

Liz blushed. 'An old one, but I don't wear it very often.' She'd told herself it wasn't for Benedict's benefit that she'd decided to put it on, but who was she kidding? His compliment had given her a warm, fuzzy feeling.

'I'M TELLING YOU IT'S THEM MASONS. OR I'M A MONKEY'S UNCLE.'

'Nah. He's on a plane. New identity, new life.'

The volume of the room dropped suddenly as Deborah Grogan came in, accompanied by Gregory and Gillian. The singers might be gossips, but they weren't cruel. Liz saw that Deborah had shadows under her carefully made-up eyes. She was surprised to see her there at all, if she was honest. She must have known she was likely to be the centre of attention.

Gregory clapped his hands. 'Come on, people, let's make a start. First of all, a big thank you to Reverend Garraway, who's given us permission to use the church for all our practice sessions until Christmas Eve. She's had quite a job persuading the police to let us in tonight.'

His words sent another ripple of speculation through the singers. There was no sign of any police presence in the church, or of the cancelled funeral service. The trestles and the flowers – like Neil Grogan himself – had gone.

Gregory waited for the murmurs to die down. 'I think we

should all also extend our gratitude to Deborah, who's agreed to accompany us in spite of upsetting personal circumstances.'

There was a murmur of approval and a smattering of applause. Deborah took her seat at the piano and shuffled her sheet music.

'I'll leave you all to it,' said Gillian. Before she retreated, a look passed between her and Benedict. It was fleeting and ambiguous, but Liz saw it. Her heart dropped into her boots.

'Take a seat, everyone. I suggest we all keep our coats on, as it isn't very warm in here. We don't want anyone to catch a cold before the big night, do we?' Gregory shuffled through his music and put it on the stand he'd brought with him. 'Let's start with "God Rest Ye".'

He tapped the stand with his baton.

Deborah played the intro.

'God rest ye merry gentlemen, let nothing you dismay.'

'GOD REST YE MERRY GENTLEMEN, LET NOTHING YOU DISMAY.'

'For Jesus Christ our saviour was born on Christmas day.'

'FOR JESUS CHRIST OUR SAVIOUR WAS BORN ON CHRISTMAS DAY.'

9

'I hear Iris is causing quite a stir at your choir.' Kevin dunked a biscuit into his tea.

'One way of putting it,' said Liz.

'Hasn't anyone tried to have a word with her?'

'I doubt there's much point. I don't think she could adjust her volume if she wanted to. And no one wants to upset her. She enjoys it so much.'

'Gregory Willis is thinking about cancelling the carol service.'

That was news to Liz. 'Who told you that?'

'One of my paid informers.' Kevin grinned. 'I could tell you, but his life would be in danger.'

'Very funny. I hope Gregory doesn't cancel, though. Everyone's worked so hard.' Liz took a sip of her own tea. 'Talking of which, how's your investigation going into the mayor's disappearance?'

'Not great.' Kevin looked glum. 'He's just vanished into thin air. But Flint won't give up.' He gave Liz a sly look. 'Your name has been mentioned a few times.'

'Mine?' She was startled. 'Why?'

'She thinks it's strange you were up at the church the night he went AWOL.'

'So was your dad.'

'Yes... but he doesn't have your reputation.'

'Reputation?'

'For trouble. Flint's sure you have something to do with it.'

Liz harrumphed. 'Just like her, barking up the wrong tree.'

'Well, we're running out of trees. We've spoken to everyone we can think of – Gillian, the family, the undertakers. Flint's even had us all at the fish market.'

'Fish market?'

'They have big refrigerators down there. Perfect for storing a body.'

'That's clutching at straws, isn't it?'

'There isn't really anything else to clutch at,' said Kevin.

'And what's happening with Mags? Do you know?'

'We're not prosecuting. There isn't enough evidence of criminal negligence. But Carolyn Grogan's still determined to bring a civil suit.'

'Poor Mags.'

'I haven't seen her since the party. How is she?'

'I don't really know. I haven't seen much of her either. I might pop along to the café this morning.'

'Good idea.'

Liz put her mug down thoughtfully. 'Just as a matter of interest, who are Grogan's undertakers?'

'Carlyle's, at Sandsend. Why?'

Liz shrugged. 'Just curious.'

THE BUS RIDE TO SANDSEND, just three miles along the coast, took less than fifteen minutes. Although the temperature hadn't risen much above freezing, it was a beautifully bright day, sharp and crisp. The sun, sitting low on the horizon, glittered off the North Sea, so that Liz had to squint against the glare as the bus trundled along. Just as they came into the village, they passed the Grogans' house on the left, set back on the hillside. It was a low modern building, with an immaculately manicured, rather utilitarian garden and huge windows that Liz guessed would offer spectacular views. She craned her neck as they passed. There were no signs of life apart from the Range Rover parked in the driveway.

She got off the bus after the narrow bridge over Sandsend Beck. Sandsend had originally been two villages, but was now combined into a single one that sprawled along the shoreline. It wasn't huge in terms of population or amenities – it only had a few hotels and restaurants – but it punched well above its weight in terms of money and influence. Liz checked her phone for directions. She turned left off the main road and followed a side road that led down the hill to a single-storey Victorian building that looked as if it used to be a community hall or school at some time. The three hearses lined up in the car park told Liz she'd reached her destination, even before she saw the sign that said '*Thos. Carlyle Funeral Directors. We grieve with you.*'

She went inside. The waiting room was thickly carpeted, but the air felt stale. There were a couple of potted plants, half a dozen spindly Victorian chairs, and a counter with a glazed hatch. Liz approached the counter. The stack of leaflets there were unintentionally comic –

Your loved one is dead. Now what?

She could see no one in the small room on the other side of the glass. She spotted a button and pushed it. A bell rang somewhere inside the building. After a few moments, a young woman dressed in dark clothes and glasses appeared in the room on the other side of the hatch. She brushed biscuit crumbs off her chest before sliding the window open.

'Good morning,' she said in hushed tones. 'Do you have an appointment?'

'No. I—'

'When did your dearly departed depart?'

'I don't want to arrange a funeral. I'd like to have a word with someone about Neil Grogan.'

The receptionist frowned. 'Are you with the police?' She spoke at normal volume.

Liz shook her head. 'No, just a family friend.'

'Mr Carlyle, our director, isn't in the office this morning. Maybe you can come back later?'

'That's not really convenient. Isn't there someone else I could talk to? Maybe someone who prepared his body for the funeral?'

'What's your name?'

'Mrs McLuckie.'

'Hold on a moment. I'll ask.' The receptionist disappeared again into the bowels of the building. After a moment or two she reappeared, but this time in the doorway of the waiting area.

'This way, please.'

Liz followed her down a corridor.

'Liz! What a lovely surprise.' To her immense astonishment Irwin Gladwell threw one of the doors open as they approached. He was wearing latex gloves and a plastic apron over his Fair Isle sweater. He ushered her into the room.

'Come in, come in. Take a seat. Hang on a minute. Let me get rid of these.' He stripped off his gloves and apron and bundled them into a surgical waste bin.

The room was fully tiled, with a drain in the middle of the floor. Liz glanced nervously at the stainless-steel table.

'Ah, don't worry, our player today has just exited the stage. He's back in the wings until his final performance.'

'I had no idea you were a mortician.' She'd known Irwin since the summer, but had never thought to ask him what he did for a living.

'I started out in theatre as a make-up artist, but the work wasn't very reliable, so I retrained. I've been here almost twenty years. Much more consistent.' Irwin winked. 'Death and taxes.' He sat on a stool beside her. 'Louise tells me you're asking about Mr Grogan. Are you sleuthing again?'

'I don't know if you've heard, but his wife is suing Mags.'

Irwin nodded. 'Bad business.'

'Someone swapped the oil that Mags had prepared for sesame oil. Maybe the same person who stole his body. If I can find out who, we can clear Mags's name.'

'How can I help?'

'It's a bit of a long shot, but did you prepare his... um... cavities?'

Irwin's eyebrows rose.

'Sorry,' continued Liz. 'I don't know exactly what you do here. But I was wondering if there might be anything hidden inside him, in his stomach, or... elsewhere.'

'Ah. I see what you're getting at. You're looking for a motive for the theft.'

'Exactly.'

'Sorry to disappoint, but if there had been anything inside Neil Grogan, the coroner's post-mortem would have found it. They eviscerate the body.'

'Oh.'

'Do you have another theory? A plan B?'

'Not really. I'm a bit stumped, if I'm honest.' A thought occurred to her. 'What do you use on your clients, by way of chemicals and cosmetics?'

'A mix of formaldehyde, glutaraldehyde, and methanol.

Then wound filler if I need it, and non-thermogenic make-up.'

'Can I smell them?'

Irwin's eyebrows almost disappeared into his hairline. 'Dare I ask why?'

'There was a smell in the church the night Grogan went missing. I'm wondering if it was traces of the body itself or something else. Something the body thief might have brought with them. It's a process of elimination, really.'

'Intriguing.' He went to a cabinet and took out a large plastic demijohn and a leopard-skin vanity case. He unscrewed the lid from the demijohn and lifted it for Liz to sniff.

'Ew!' Liz recoiled and put her hand over her nose. 'Pickled apples. That's not it.'

Irwin resealed the demijohn and put it back in the cabinet. 'I didn't have to use wound filler on Mr Grogan, thankfully, just make-up.' He opened the vanity case, selected a few bottles and tubes and held them up, one by one, to Liz's nose.

She shook her head. 'Not them either.'

'Are you sure it wasn't just decomposition? All the embalming fluid in the world can't mask it completely.'

'I don't think so.' As an ex-nurse, she was quite familiar with that smell. But she was running out of options. Then she remembered something else she'd wanted to ask.

'Carolyn Grogan used an EpiPen, but it didn't work. Was there a puncture wound on the body?'

'You're thinking she might have just pretended to use it? Well, if there was a puncture wound, I doubt it would have been visible to the naked eye. And even if it was, Grogan was a hirsute chap. It would be like looking for a needle in a haystack.' He looked thoughtful. 'But even if she did use the EpiPen, that doesn't mean it actually contained epinephrine, does it?'

'What else might have been in it?'

Irwin shrugged. 'Saline?'

'I never thought of that.' Liz fell silent, thinking. Someone could have swapped the EpiPen, the same as they had the cooking oil. Things were getting really murky now and potentially very complicated. Who could have had access to the oil and the EpiPen? Presumably Carolyn Grogan had kept the pen in her bag or her pocket. It had to be someone close to her. Or Carolyn herself.

Irwin was watching her closely. 'Penny for them?'

'I'm not sure they're worth that much, Irwin. Thanks for your help, though.'

'Any time. I don't like the idea of Mags getting sued any more than you do. She's a lovely lady. If there's anything else I can do, just let me know.'

Liz nodded and headed for the door. 'We missed you at choir last night.'

'My client yesterday took longer than expected. Car accident.'

Liz grimaced. 'Sorry to hear that.' She wondered whether to broach the subject of Iris's singing, and decided not to. She'd tested Irwin's patience enough for one day.

AFTER LIZ GOT off the bus at Whitby bus station, she went straight to the Full Moon Café. It was empty apart from Grazyna, who was reading a newspaper at one of the tables. She looked up when the door tinkled.

'Thank God, a customer. Even if it is only you.'

'Thanks a lot.'

'Do not mention it. Your usual?'

'Please. And a scone if you have one.'

Liz sat down as Grazyna went behind the counter to make the tea.

'Has it been this quiet all day?'

'All week. Like a graveyard.'

'Hello.' Mags emerged through the curtain. 'I thought I heard the door.' Her face was pale, her eyes smudged with shadows. She sat at the table beside Liz.

'How are you doing?' asked Liz.

'Oh, I'm great. Fabulous.' She gestured at the empty café. 'Being this busy has really taken my mind off things.'

Liz frowned. It wasn't like Mags to be sarcastic.

Mags caught Liz's expression, and her eyes welled with tears. 'Sorry.'

'Kevin told me the police aren't going to get involved.'

'No. That's something, I suppose.'

'If they don't have enough evidence for a criminal prosecution, surely they don't have enough for a civil one?'

'My lawyer says it doesn't work like that.'

'You are going to fight it though?'

'I suppose. I'm just not sure how.'

Grazyna brought Liz her tea and scone and joined them at the table. In the face of Mags's misery, Liz didn't feel like eating anymore, but she feigned enthusiasm and smothered her scone with cream and jam.

'Someone told me they saw Adam Grogan in the kitchen at the party,' she said to Mags. 'I don't suppose you saw him there?'

Mags frowned, trying to remember. 'Not that I... oh, hang on a minute... yes! I'd been out to get something I'd left in the van, and when I came back, I bumped into him at the door. He told me he was looking for the gents', which I thought was odd, because it's on the other side of the museum.'

'The filthy хорек,' hissed Grazyna. 'He swapped the oil!'

Liz had no idea what a хорек was, and thought that was probably for the best. But she didn't want Grazyna to embrace Adam's guilt without evidence.

'We don't know that,' she said; then she turned to Mags. 'Can you remember if he was carrying anything?'

'No, I don't think so.'

'Perhaps he had already done it?' suggested Grazyna.

'Do you think we should tell the police?' asked Mags.

Liz shook her head. 'Adam being in the kitchen isn't proof of anything. But it's a start.'

'Forget police,' sneered Grazyna. 'The only thing you can rely on are these.' She lifted her hands and made them into fists. Liz had a sudden alarming vision of Adam Grogan being shivved in some dark corner of the town.

'We need hard evidence, Grazyna. We need the police on our side. We have to clear Mags's name.'

'So what do we do next?' asked Mags.

Liz thought about it. 'I'll have a word with him. He might say something that gives us more to go on.'

'Good plan.' Grazyna nodded in satisfaction. 'Evidence first... *then...*' She balled her hands into fists again.

10

L iz sniffed her jogging pants experimentally. She hadn't done any serious exercise since Mark had first taken ill seven years ago. When she'd moved to Whitby she'd brought her exercise gear with her, telling herself she would take up running or classes again, but of course she hadn't. She found her sports bag tucked away with some other things she still hadn't unpacked at the back of the attic cupboard in Gull Cottage. Her leggings, sports bra and trainers were faded, shapeless, and smelled musty, but she didn't have time to put them through the washing machine. She had an appointment at four thirty.

She'd called Shapeshifters Gym as soon as she'd got home from the café.

'Hello, I was wondering if you had a step class this afternoon.'

'*A what?*'

'A step class.'

The receptionist made a stifled noise that could have been a snigger. '*No. We have cross training at six thirty tonight, or a spin class at eight.*'

Liz wondered what a spin class was, and decided it was too risky to sign up for one when she had no idea what it might involve.

'Maybe I'll just pop in and use the gym instead,' she said.

'*Are you a member?*' asked the girl.

'No.'

'*You can't just "pop in". You have to have an induction first.*'

'I have used a gym before.'

'*When was that, exactly?*'

Liz was silent. She didn't want to say.

'*Our machines are state of the art. You need to come in for an induction and then sign up as a member.*'

'How much does it cost?'

'*We have three different packages. They start at thirty pounds a month, plus a joining fee.*'

Liz stifled a yelp, but forced herself to continue. 'I know it's very last minute, but I don't suppose you could fit me in for an induction this afternoon?'

'*I doubt it. Mr Grogan likes to do them himself, and he's very busy.*'

There was a pause.

'Could you check, please?' prompted Liz, trying not to let irritation get the better of her.

The receptionist sighed. '*Hang on.*'

Liz waited. If they couldn't fit her in that afternoon, she would just have to doorstep Adam Grogan, but it would be much better if she just happened to 'bump into' him, and could engineer the conversation naturally. She'd been meaning to start exercising again, and this could be the push she needed. Thirty pounds a month was steep, but would be worth it if it stopped her from slumping into a decrepit old age.

The receptionist came back on the line. '*You're in luck. He's had a cancellation at four thirty.*'

'Perfect. My name's Liz McLuckie. I'll see you then.'

A COUPLE of hours later Liz stared at her reflection in one of the many, many mirrors in the changing rooms. She was the same weight she'd been at twenty-one, but in the intervening thirty years, everything had emigrated south. With decent underwear, flattering clothing and make-up, she could still brush up well, but in the harsh lighting of the changing room, with her curly chestnut hair – her only real claim to beauty – scraped into a scrunchie, she both looked and felt her age. She was glad the gym wasn't busy.

'Get a grip,' she muttered to her reflection. 'Faint heart never won fair lady.'

She went into the gym.

Adam Grogan was waiting for her beside one of the daunting-looking machines. When she'd seen him at St Mary's, he'd been wearing his winter clothes, and she'd thought he was quite bulky. Now he was in Lycra, however, it was clear all that bulk was muscle. He had a masculine but pleasant face, with rosy cheeks. She had to admit he didn't look much like a murderer. But, as she knew only all too well, killers came in all shapes and sizes.

'Mrs McLuckie?' He clearly hadn't recognised her from St Mary's, which was a good thing. His bicep bulged as he shook her hand.

'Liz,' she said. She tried not to flinch as he ran a critical eye over her body.

'What exactly do you want to achieve from your exercise regime?'

'Well... you know, just tone everything up a bit.'

He nodded encouragingly. 'It's never too late to start, is it?'

Ouch.

'We'll do an easy one first,' he said. He went to one of the machines. 'This is the erg.'

It looked like a rowing machine to Liz. A rowing machine crossed with a laptop.

'It looks pretty scary, but it's easy to use, and it's great for pretty much everything – quads, hamstrings, glutes, lats, core, shoulders, triceps, back and biceps.'

He settled Liz onto the machine. Her palms still stung from her run-in with Dora, and she struggled to get a firm grip on the handles.

'The trick is to push with your legs first, then lean backwards so your shoulders pass your pelvis. Pull your arms toward your chest, right at your lower ribs. That's right. We'll give you five minutes on this, and then I'll be back to see how you're doing. Okay?'

Liz nodded. He gave her an encouraging pat on her shoulder, then left her to her own devices.

She gave up after three minutes. While she was trying to get her breath back, she wondered how she was going to bring the conversation round to the council party. Perhaps a direct approach was the least suspicious?

Adam returned, as promised, when the five minutes were up.

'How was that?'

'Great.'

He glanced at the screen and frowned. 'Okay. Maybe we'll try the chest press next.'

She didn't like the sound of that. He led her to another machine.

'I was really sorry to hear about your father,' she blurted.

Adam kept his eyes firmly on the new machine. 'This will work your pecs, deltoids, traps and triceps and give you the strength you need to take on more intense workouts in the future.' He adjusted the weights.

She wondered if he'd heard her. 'His death must have been a shock for you all.'

He looked at her, but said nothing.

'And for it to happen in public like that,' she plunged on. 'Terrible.'

He nodded curtly. 'You need to lie back on the bench and position your arms slightly farther than shoulder width apart.'

At a loss what to say next, she obeyed.

'Just grasp the bar, and move your arms up and down, like you're doing push-ups. That's it. Three sets of ten reps to start. I'll count for you.'

Liz started.

'One... two... three...'

By the time they got to thirty, her arms and chest were burning. She sat up again, feeling a little wobbly.

'Were you there?' she asked. 'At the council party?'

'You know what?' said Adam. 'You look as if you could do another set of ten. Shall we give it a go?'

By the time her induction was finished, Liz could barely totter back to the changing room. She'd punished every single muscle group, but was no further in her quest to find out what Adam had been up to in the kitchen on the night of his father's death. She'd continued to probe as they'd moved from one instrument of torture to the next, but he had ignored every single gambit. In the end she'd given up. It was all she could do to concentrate on her aching body and burning lungs.

Adam was nowhere to be seen when she came out of the changing rooms.

'How did you get on?' asked the receptionist. It was the same girl she'd spoken to on the phone.

'Not too bad.'

'I can take your membership details now, if you like.'

Talk about preying on the weak.

'You know what,' countered Liz, 'I'm a little pooped. I'll call you about it tomorrow, if that's okay?'

The girl gave her a sceptical look, but nodded.

Liz headed out into the darkness. Shapeshifters Gym was on the west side of town, only a twenty-minute walk from home, but she wasn't sure she was going to make it back. She felt a bit light-headed.

'Liz!' A cyclist pulled up at the kerb beside her with a squeak of brakes. It was Benedict, on his road bike, in his Lycra and helmet. He was sweating.

'I thought it was you,' he gasped. 'Been somewhere nice?'

'The gym.' She was suddenly acutely conscious of her own red face and lack of make-up.

'Really?'

She pushed down her irritation. Why was he so surprised?

'I'll walk with you.' He swung his leg off his bike. 'I've had enough for tonight anyway.'

As he took off his helmet, Liz realised that something was penetrating her exhaustion and self-consciousness. When she realised what it was, she stiffened and clutched Benedict's arm.

'What?' He peered at her, concerned. 'Are you okay?'

She nodded and sniffed again, just to be sure.

'What is it?'

'It's you!'

'Chamois cream. We use it to stop chafing,' said Benedict as he handed her a mug of tea in his toasty kitchen. 'The main ingredient is witch hazel.'

Liz sniffed the jar again. 'Dad used to put witch hazel on our bruises. It's definitely the same smell as in St Mary's. I knew I recognised it, but couldn't put my finger on what it was exactly.'

'I'd have recognised it myself if my nose hadn't been so bunged up.'

'Whoever took Neil Grogan's body smelled of witch hazel.'

'Could they be a cyclist?' Benedict rubbed the back of his neck thoughtfully. Then his eyes widened. 'Guiseppe Ricci!'

Liz frowned. 'Who?'

'Neil Grogan's son-in-law. Helen's husband. He's a member of my cycling club.' Benedict looked at her earnestly. 'What do you think? Could it be a coincidence?'

'Maybe.' Liz sipped her tea. 'But it's certainly worth looking into.'

'I have no idea where they live.'

'They can't be too hard to find. I don't suppose there are a lot of Riccis in Whitby.'

'THIS IS IT, I THINK.' Benedict parked his BMW in front of number thirty-two Maid Marion Avenue, a detached house on a modern estate on the outskirts of town. 'Are you sure you don't want me to come with you?'

Liz shook her head. 'I don't think we should go in mob-handed.'

'Then let me do it.'

'With respect, you can be a bit intimidating. They're more likely to lower their guard with me.'

Benedict nodded, acknowledging her point. 'Well, please be careful.'

'I will.' She opened the passenger door. 'I'll call you later. Let you know how it goes.'

Benedict scowled. 'What are you talking about? You don't think I'm just going to leave you here? You must have a really low opinion of me if you think that.'

'But I don't know how long I'll be.'

'It doesn't matter. I'll be waiting.'

That thought warmed her as she went up the path. It was a big, detached house with a garage and a plastic swing set on the front lawn. There was a slightly battered estate car parked on the driveway. As she passed, she saw there was a baby seat in the back, strewn with tissues, packets of baby wipes, and empty juice cartons. The messiness of the car interior was at odds with the well-kept lawn and borders.

Helen Ricci, Neil Grogan's daughter, answered the door. She was wearing jeans and a sweatshirt with a stain on the front. She looked just as pale as she had in the church, and even more exhausted.

'Liz McLuckie.' Liz held out her hand. 'We met briefly at St Mary's. Reverend Garraway has asked me to come and see how you are getting on.'

'Oh.' Helen blinked. 'That's very nice of her. Very nice of you.'

'The last couple of days must have been very hard.'

Helen hesitated, but politeness prevailed.

'Um... come in.' She opened the door wider.

'Thanks.' Liz had thought that would be more difficult. Thank heavens for good manners. As she went into the hall, a small, shaggy terrier jumped up to greet her with a bark.

'Shhhh. Shut up, you daft thing,' Helen soothed it. 'We don't get many people calling at this time,' she explained to Liz. 'The kids are in bed.'

'I can go if I'm disturbing you?'

'No, it's fine.' Helen led her into the living room and cleared some toys and books off a chair for Liz to sit. The terrier stood on his hind legs to put his chin on Liz's knee.

'Don't mind Truffle. He's just being nosy.'

'He can probably smell my dog.' Liz felt a twinge of guilt as she petted the terrier. Poor Nelson had been left on his own too much the last few days. She would have to make it up to him somehow.

'Sorry about the mess,' said Helen, dumping her armful of stuff onto another chair. 'I'm not usually so disorganised.'

Something in the pile caught Liz's eye – a single, rainbow-coloured baby sock. She'd seen one like it before.

'Would you like a cup of tea? I was just about to put the kettle on.'

'I'm fine, thanks.'

Liz's brain was working overtime. How had that sock's twin come to be in St Mary's car park? Perhaps it had it accidentally fallen out of Helen's car – Liz had seen how messy it was in there. But Helen's car hadn't been at the church that night. Helen hadn't driven there herself, she'd gone in Carolyn Grogan's Range Rover. If the sock had fallen out of Helen's car, it had to have been in the car park at some point before that.

Liz scanned the shelves, which were lined with family photos. There were several of Helen with a smiling, black-haired man. Probably Guiseppe, her husband.

'Is your husband at work?'

'He's upstairs, in bed. He isn't very well at the moment.'

'Nothing serious, I hope?'

'He hurt his back a couple of days ago.'

Lifting something heavy?

Liz looked at the photos again. As well as photos of Helen, Guiseppe and their children, there were several of Neil Grogan, some with Deborah and some on his own. There were none at all of Carolyn, not even a recent wedding photo.

'How is your stepmother coping?'

'She's fine.' Helen's lips drew into a grim, weary line. 'Carolyn's always fine.'

Something in her tone made Liz frown. 'Do you think she killed him?'

'What?' Helen's eyes flickered with alarm.

'Do you think she engineered the allergic reaction?'

Helen squared her shoulders. 'I wouldn't put it past her. God knows what was in that EpiPen, but it wasn't epinephrine.'

'I think he was murdered too,' said Liz. 'I just don't know who did it.'

'She did.'

'What makes you think that?'

'She's twenty years younger than Dad. Twenty years! That's the same age as Adam... Dad didn't have the chance to make another will after they got married. She gets everything.'

'You think she planned it?'

'Right from the start. But I can't prove it. The post-mortem didn't find anything... but, there again, they weren't looking for foul play.'

'And a second autopsy wouldn't be possible if the body was cremated?'

'No.'

There was a long pause while they stared at each other. Helen broke first.

'He's in the garage.'

Liz didn't know what to say. Even though it was what she suspected, having it confirmed was still a shock.

'I wasn't thinking properly,' blurted Helen. 'I was so upset, and I knew Carolyn would never agree to another autopsy. I persuaded Guiseppe to help. We sneaked into the vestry at the church and put bisacodyl into the reverend's flask. Then we took Dad. He was much heavier than we thought.'

'Guiseppe hurt himself?'

'Pretty badly, I think. But he won't let me call the doctor, in case someone puts two and two together, like you did.' Helen's face crumpled, and she sobbed. Truffle, the terrier, whined and pawed at her leg. Helen lifted him up and hugged him to her chest for comfort. 'I don't know what we were thinking.'

'What are you going to do now?'

'I have no idea. I don't know anyone who would do an illegal autopsy – I never thought that far ahead. And there's been such an uproar about Dad going missing... I don't want to go to prison. I don't want Guiseppe to go to prison.'

'I'm not sure it would come to that.'

Helen wiped her eyes with her sleeve. 'Detective Inspector Flint says whoever took Dad is guilty of trespass, theft, and obstruction of justice. But I don't see any way around it. We're going to have to come clean.'

Liz looked at her. She was the picture of misery, her face streaked with tears, hugging her little terrier to her stained sweatshirt. Liz decided she didn't want Helen to go to prison either.

12

The wind woke Liz in the middle of the night. She snuggled back under her duvet, listening to it nag and quarrel with the scree on the cliff above her, hoping no more tiles would be broken. She was desperate to start renting Kipper out again, but everything seemed to be going backwards. She twisted and turned, trying to go back to sleep, but thoughts of her mounting repair bills kept intruding. Then, inevitably, she started to think about the shocking revelations of the previous day.

She hadn't told Benedict what she and Helen had spoken about, or that Neil Grogan's body was lying in Helen Ricci's garage. She'd just said that Helen had been very nice, but hadn't been able to offer any explanation for the smell of witch hazel in the church. Guiseppe was ill and couldn't have been involved in the theft of Neil Grogan's body. She felt awful lying to him, but knew she was doing the right thing. She wanted to help Helen if she could, but didn't need to drag Benedict into it. It wasn't fair.

She couldn't go back to sleep. At six o'clock she gave in and got up. She got dressed and then took a delighted Nelson

for an early morning walk around the empty streets. She
loved the town when there was no one else about. She ended
up sitting in glorious solitude on a bench at Pannet Park just
as the rising sun painted the underbelly of the clouds a rosy
pink. She took out her phone.

'Liz!' Kevin was surprised. 'You're up early. I've just started
my shift.'

'I didn't sleep very well last night. How did you get on
with your enquiries into Neil Grogan's will?'

'His solicitor wasn't very forthcoming. I could have strong-
armed him, but not without Flint finding out.'

'It doesn't matter. He died without making a new will
after he got married. Carolyn Grogan gets everything.'

'Interesting.'

'Isn't it?'

'And yet...' Kevin sounded thoughtful.

'What?'

'If Carolyn killed him, I'm not sure that sits well with her
pursuing Mags in the courts for negligence. If it were me, I'd be
wanting to move on from the whole thing as quickly as possible.'

He did have a point. 'How are things going with you and
Anna?'

'Erm...' He hesitated, wrong-footed by her sudden change
of subject. 'Okay, I suppose. I haven't actually seen her since the
night at Dad's.'

'Would you mind if I gave her a call? I'd like to ask her
about something.'

'About Neil Grogan? I could do it if you like?'

'Isn't it better for you to keep your work and love life
separate?'

'I suppose. Although I'm not sure it would make much
difference.'

Liz deduced that the romance wasn't going as well as he'd
have liked.

'Is everything okay with you two?' she asked.

'I don't know. We're both so busy, working long hours, and our shifts often clash. But, yeah. I think it'll be fine... I'll text you her number. Let me know if you find out anything.'

Liz headed home before she made the call.

'Hello?' Anna reacted warily to the unknown number.

'Hi, Anna. It's Liz here. Liz McLuckie. We met the other night? I got your number from Kevin.'

'Oh. How are you?'

'Great, thanks. Listen, I'm sorry to bother you at work like this. I have a professional question.'

There was a beat of surprise. *'Okay. Fire away.'*

'Is it possible to tell post-mortem if an EpiPen has been used?'

There was a pause on the other end of the line. *'Well... it's complicated. Adrenaline does show up post-mortem. Cate-cholamines and metanephrines can be measured in peripheral and cardiac blood as well as urine and vitreous humour. But everyone has natural levels of adrenaline in their body, especially if they've experienced ante-mortem stress.'*

'So... there's no sure way of knowing?'

'Not really. Plus, there's the added complication that adrenaline breaks down at low temperatures. So if the body has been chilled at all...' She broke off. *'I assume we're talking about Neil Grogan?'*

'Yes.'

'His body would have been chilled before and after his PM. Even if there were unusually high levels of adrenaline immediately after he died, it wouldn't necessarily show up in the toxicology report.'

'Ah. That's a pity. Thanks anyway.'

'Any time.'

'I really enjoyed meeting you the other night. I hope we see more of you.'

'Me too.' But Anna sounded doubtful. Liz wasn't sure

whether to say anything else, but decided not to. She really had to curb her busybody tendencies.

When she'd got off the phone, Liz was thoughtful. There really wasn't any point in Helen hanging on to her father's body if there was no way of being able to tell if he'd been the victim of foul play. Helen would have to confess to the police what she and Guiseppe had done. That would have serious repercussions.

Unless...

13

Helen Ricci picked up Liz and Tilly at the swing bridge at 2 am. The night was beyond cold – the lowest temperature they'd seen so far that winter. The sky was clear, and the moon haloed with frost.

'I've put him in a sheet,' said Helen as she drove them to her house. 'He'll be easier to carry that way.'

'Good thinking,' said Liz.

Tilly just grunted. She had been incredulous when Liz had approached her.

'You want me to help you *unsteal* Neil Grogan's body?'

'I wouldn't get you involved, but Guiseppe's hurt his back. Helen and I can't manage him on our own. Plus... we have to break into the church.'

'Can't you just leave him somewhere else?'

'Where? At least there's a car park at the church and no cameras.'

'Why do you have to break in? Can't you just dump him in the graveyard?'

'There's no saying how long it would take for someone to

find him. And it just seems disrespectful. I doubt Helen would want to do that.'

She hadn't. Although she'd been beyond grateful when Liz and Tilly had offered their help, she'd insisted they should put her father back in the church.

In the car, Liz shivered. She'd dressed in her exercise gear again, for ease of movement, but was already regretting it. Even though she was also wearing a sweater, a padded jacket, and her nice new gloves, she was still freezing. 'Can you turn the heating up a bit?'

'Isn't it best not to? Under the circumstances?'

It took a moment for Liz to realise what Helen was getting at. 'Ah. You might be right.'

There was a very unpleasant odour in the garage that Liz knew all too well from her years working in hospitals. Even though it was cold in there, nature had taken its inevitable course.

The three women looked down at Neil Grogan's body. Helen had wrapped him in a dark green sheet and wound garden twine around him to keep the sheet in place. He looked like a badly made dolma. Liz felt an entirely inappropriate urge to giggle. She supposed it was a stress response.

'Best get on with it,' said Tilly, without enthusiasm. 'I'll take the feet if you two take the heavy end.'

Having the body in a sheet definitely made it easier to carry, but it was still something of a struggle to slide it into Helen's estate car. They drove in silence to St Mary's. As they'd expected, the car park was empty, and there were no lights on either at the museum or in the church itself. Thanks to the moonlight, they didn't need the torches they'd brought with them. Tilly rummaged through her bag of tools and found her favourite crowbar.

'This should do it. You two wait here. I'll tell you when I'm in.'

Liz and Tilly knew that a storeroom window had been broken at the back of the church in the summer, during one of their previous adventures. Tilly was counting on it not having been repaired. It was a fairly safe bet. Gillian was always complaining about how difficult it was for the church committee to sanction anything that needed fixing.

Helen and Liz waited. Having a corpse in the car with them wasn't conducive to conversation, and they were both nervous. After what felt like hours, but was probably only a few minutes, they saw a dark figure scramble back over the car park wall. They got out of the car.

Liz's heart was thumping in her chest, but Tilly looked as if she were out for an afternoon stroll.

'All done,' she said matter-of-factly. 'I've unlocked the main door from the inside. The only problem is that the gate is padlocked. We'll have to take him over the wall.'

That wasn't good news. It had been hard enough to lift him into the car. Liz and Helen looked at each other in dismay.

'No point making a drama out of it,' said Tilly. 'We've just got to do it.'

They opened the boot and dragged the body out. The weight caused the sheet to slip through Liz's gloved fingers, and it fell with a horrible 'flump' onto the tarmac. Helen looked as if she was going to be sick.

'Sorry,' said Liz.

They picked their burden up again and carried it with difficulty to the stone wall.

'Head first, I think,' said Tilly. They manoeuvred the body around so it was pointing in the other direction.

'One, two, three.'

They strained to lift it to shoulder height.

'Push.'

They pushed as hard as they could, and managed to slide the head and shoulders over the wall.

'Okay,' hissed Tilly through gritted teeth. 'Hold him there.'

Liz and Helen held their position while Tilly hoisted herself over the wall. Liz could feel her muscles burning. If Helen and Guiseppe had had to take Neil over the wall when they'd stolen him, they wouldn't have made it. Which would have saved everyone a *lot* of trouble.

With Tilly pulling and Helen and Liz pushing, they finally managed to get Neil Grogan over the wall and onto the long grass on the other side. Liz and Helen scrambled over the wall to join Tilly.

'Great,' whispered Tilly. 'We're nearly there.'

That was wishful thinking. It was at least a hundred yards to the church, and the mayor's body seemed to get heavier with every step they took. Eventually they reached the main door and pushed it open. Their eyes took a few seconds to adjust to the darker interior, but, thanks to the moon, they could still see where they were going.

'Where shall we put him?' asked Liz.

'Where the coffin was, if you don't mind?' said Helen.

'Why not?' muttered Tilly.

They staggered down the aisle and laid their burden on the stone flags where the trestles had stood.

'We should take him out of the sheet,' said Tilly.

'Really?' Helen was dismayed.

'The less physical evidence we leave, the better.'

Tilly was right. It *was* quite a distinctive sheet. Tilly took a penknife from her pocket and cut the garden twine. They had to lift the body to unwrap it, which was easier said than done. Liz had to take her gloves off to get a proper grip on the sheet. In the end they just tugged the sheet hard. Neil Grogan rolled across the floor, like Cleopatra from her carpet. He came to rest face down, several feet away from where they had intended.

'I can't leave him like that,' said Helen.

They turned him over. Liz was careful not to look at his face. She hoped their manhandling hadn't undone too much of Irwin's good work, but really didn't want to check.

'Done,' said Tilly. 'Let's go.'

Helen hesitated. Moonlight glittered on her wet cheeks. Tilly softened. She put her arm around Helen's shoulders and hugged her.

'I'm sorry. But we really have to go.'

Helen nodded and wiped her face. When they got outside, Liz took a deep breath of freezing air. They started back towards the wall.

'WHO IS THAT?' The beam of a torch swung towards them – someone had come up the abbey steps and was walking along the path to the church. They all ducked behind a gravestone.

'IS SOMEONE THERE?'

Liz recognised Gillian's voice.

'We'll have to run for it,' muttered Tilly. 'Don't look back. Don't let her see your face.'

They leapt out from behind the gravestone and set off at a run for the car park wall. The beam of Gillian's torch swung round to follow them as they tore through the long grass, dodging gravestones.

'STOP!'

Tilly vaulted the wall first, and then Liz scrambled over it, fuelled by adrenaline. Liz gave Helen her hand to help her over. They made it to the car in Olympic time. Gillian wasn't quite so fast. Helen gunned the car out of the car park just as she started over the wall. When Liz looked back through the rear window, she saw the beam of Gillian's torch drop as she landed on her feet.

'Do you think she saw the car properly?' gasped Helen. 'The number plate?'

'I don't think so.' Tilly shook her head. 'We were too far away.'

Liz could feel something churning inside her. A bubble of laughter burst between her lips.

Tilly grinned at her over her shoulder. 'This'll be a story to tell the grandkids, eh?'

Liz giggled.

Helen looked affronted. 'Not one I'll be sharing with mine, thank you very much.'

Tilly and Liz fell silent, appalled by their own insensitivity. But as Helen stared at the road ahead of her, her mouth slowly curved into a smile.

'I think Guiseppe will enjoy it though.'

They all surrendered to laughter. It had a distinct note of hysteria.

When their giggles and hiccups had subsided, Liz shivered. Now the adrenaline was wearing off, she was starting to feel her extremities again. She rummaged through her pockets.

'Oh no,' she muttered. She checked again, just to be sure.

'What is it?' asked Tilly.

'I've lost one of my gloves.'

14

N eil Grogan's funeral took place two days later. The condition of his body had made it something of a priority, and the police saw no reason why it couldn't go ahead.

Gillian provided tea and biscuits for the Eskside Singers in the vestry before the service. Speculation and rumour ran freely.

'Perhaps the kidnappers got their money?' suggested Crystal. She was going to be playing the piano again instead of Deborah, who had decided not to accompany the singers after all, and would be sitting with the family. Liz assumed Iris had something to do with that decision.

Someone else snorted. 'I doubt it. The Grogans are a tight-fisted lot. It's more likely the kidnappers just gave up.'

'I TOLD YOU, IT WAS THE MASONS.' Iris slurped her tea. 'THEY'VE HAD THEIR FUN WITH HIM AND BROUGHT HIM BACK.'

Liz and Benedict hid their smiles.

'Were all his organs there?' asked Robert Buckle. 'Has anyone looked?'

Everyone had a different theory, but they all agreed it was very bizarre for their dead mayor to disappear and then turn up again with no explanation.

'What were you doing up there at that time of night anyway?' asked Liz to Gillian.

Gillian gave her an odd look. 'I have insomnia. Sometimes I go up to the church to pray.'

'Did you give a description to police?' asked Benedict.

'I gave them what I could, although, to be honest, it wasn't much.'

Benedict frowned. 'You say there were three of them?'

'As far as I could see.' Gillian's eyes slid to Liz, then away again. 'Excuse me. I need to go and see if anyone's arrived yet.' She went into the church.

Gillian's odd manner worried Liz. Had she recognised her? Or maybe she'd found her glove? Liz had taken Nelson up to the graveyard the next morning to look for it, and had scanned the church as unobtrusively as possible when she'd arrived. There was no sign of her lost glove. Even if Gillian had found it, that didn't necessarily mean she would know it belonged to Liz, or that it proved Liz had anything to do with returning the mayor's body. She could have lost it at any time.

Irwin offered Liz a biscuit from one of the plates and leaned in confidentially. 'Do you still think whoever took him also killed him?' he asked, *sotto voce*.

Liz was saved from having to reply by the appearance of Gregory. He clapped his hands. 'Two minutes, everyone. If anyone needs the loo, now's the time to do it.'

'I DON'T NEED A WEE. I'M LIKE A CAMEL. I CAN HOLD IT FOREVER.'

Gregory winced. 'Please try to keep the volume down, Mrs Gladwell. Less is more. Particularly at a funeral.'

'RIGHT YOU ARE, GREGORY. YOU CAN COUNT ON ME.'

Gregory looked at her in despair. Iris was nothing if not reliable.

'*You have set a boundary that they may not pass over.*'

'YOU HAVE SET A BOUNDARY THAT THEY MAY NOT PASS OVER.'

'*That they may not return to cover the earth.*'

'THAT THEY MAY NOT RETURN TO COVER THE EARTH.'

When the last note of the psalm died away, you could hear a pin drop in the church. Carolyn Grogan, Adam, Philip and Helen stared at Iris in horror. Deborah's face was stony. The rest of the mourners started to mutter amongst themselves. There was a distinct snigger somewhere near the back. Carolyn glared at Gregory, whose face was scarlet with mortification.

Everyone was relieved when Gillian brought the service to a dignified close, and everyone filed out after the coffin.

Liz and Benedict stayed where they were. 'I'm glad that's over,' said Liz, slumping in her pew.

'Are you going to the buffet?' asked Benedict. 'It's at the Regent. We've all been invited.'

'After that performance I wouldn't be surprised if the invitation was revoked.'

From an investigative point of view, Liz knew that the post-funeral buffet was the perfect opportunity to see the Grogan family dynamics in action, but she was suddenly exhausted. 'I think I'll give it a miss.'

'I'm going to drop in for ten minutes. Pay my respects. See you later?'

'Sure.'

He headed out, behind Iris and Irwin.

'I THINK THAT WENT WELL, DON'T YOU?' Iris bellowed at Benedict. He made some polite response that Liz couldn't hear. Irwin said nothing.

Liz waited until everyone else had gone, then made her way home down the abbey steps. It had been quite an afternoon.

After taking Nelson for a short walk, she curled up with him on the sofa in the sitting room. Her nocturnal adventures at the church were catching up with her. She kept forgetting that she wasn't as young as she used to be.

HER MOBILE PHONE WOKE HER. It was dark, and she was so deeply asleep that it took her a moment or two to realise what was making the noise. She wriggled her arm free from underneath Nelson and groped for her phone.

'*Liz!*' It was Tilly, her tone urgent. '*You'll never guess what's happened.*'

'What? What time is it?'

'*Seven-ish... Carolyn Grogan's dead!*'

'What?'

'*She died at the Regent. I've just heard.*'

'Oh my God.' Liz switched the lamp on. She'd slept for hours. She rubbed her eyes, trying to rouse herself. 'Are you sure?'

'*Very sure.*'

'What did she die of?'

'*A heart attack.*' Tilly hesitated. '*All I can think is that now she can't come after Mags. Does that make me an awful person?*'

MIKE, the fishmonger, confirmed it the next morning.

'Keeled over right there in the hotel lobby.' He sipped his coffee and gave a serious shake of his head, oblivious to the fact he'd brought the aroma of fish into Gull Cottage with him. Nelson's nose twitched as he lay in his basket.

'But she seemed perfectly okay at the funeral,' said Liz.

'Aye... She was a bit of a health nut, by all accounts. Always at the gym. I used to see her running sometimes, along Sandsend Road.'

'Poor thing.'

'Just goes to show,' said Mike. 'We're all living on a knife-edge. We can be going along as usual one minute, right as rain, then, BOOM! Dead as a doornail. It makes you think. *Carpe diem* and all that.'

'It does.' Liz sipped her tea, mind churning. 'Who was with Carolyn when she died, do you know?'

'Adam Grogan and his sister, from what I've heard. Although the place was packed. Everyone from the funeral was there.'

Liz knew the *Whitby Bugle* would give more details when it hit the news stands at lunchtime, but until then Mike was the next best thing. His gossiping was never malicious – he was just interested in people. Plus, of course, there wasn't anyone in town he didn't know.

'More coffee, Mike?'

He shook his head. 'Have to be on my way. I have lobsters waiting in the van.' He drained his mug and headed for the door. 'Thanks for the warm-up.' He turned in the doorway to wag a finger at her. '*Carpe diem*, Mrs Mac, *Carpe diem!*'

GULLS WHEELED and yodelled overhead as Liz made her way up the steps that led up from the harbour to the whalebone arch. The arch was a well-known Whitby landmark – the jawbone of a mighty whale that had been erected on the West Cliff sometime in the mid-eighteen hundreds, as a memorial to all the whalers in the town who had died. The crumbling bone had been replaced at some point by a resin replica, but it remained a local beauty spot, framing the view of the ruined abbey and St Mary's church on the opposite cliff. She paused under the whalebone to admire the view, and hefted her rucksack more comfortably onto her shoulders. She'd brought some of Mags's home-made sandwiches with her, as well as sausage rolls and tea in a flask. It was much too cold for a picnic, really, but she'd wanted to get some fresh air and feel the sun on her skin, even if it had no warmth to it. Because it was so cold, she'd left Nelson at home.

She'd arranged to meet Kevin in their favourite spot at one thirty, but it was almost ten to two when she saw his unmarked car pull up in the Pavilion Drive car park. He hurried to join her in the glass shelter that looked out over the North Sea.

'Sorry! You must be frozen.'

'Don't worry about it.' Liz poured them both some tea from the flask and gave him a cup as he sat on the bench beside her.

'I imagine you've been busy?' she said.

'Just a bit. I've spent the morning fielding calls about Carolyn Grogan. And it isn't as if I can tell anyone anything. The coroner always has a backlog this time of year. We'll be lucky if the post-mortem happens before the New Year.'

Liz knew he was right. It was the sixteenth of December. She unwrapped the sandwiches, trying to ignore a huge herring gull that was standing a few feet away, eyeing them beadily.

'Do you think she was murdered?' she asked.

'I don't know, to be honest.' He bit into his sandwich and spoke around it. 'It does seem a coincidence, doesn't it? But if she had a heart condition, the stress of her husband's death... then his body going missing... it makes sense.'

'Does it?'

'That's what Flint thinks. She's more bothered about investigating the theft of his body. She's blaming the body thief for Carolyn's death too.'

'That's a bit of a stretch.'

Kevin shrugged. 'For once I think she has a point... Oh. Sausage rolls. My favourite!'

Liz watched as he pounced on them. Poor Helen wasn't off the hook yet.

'I think it would be pretty hard to kill someone and make it look like a heart attack,' she mused. She made a mental note to research it.

Kevin's sausage roll disappeared in a couple of bites. He picked up another. 'Why get involved?'

That was a good question. With Mags no longer threatened with a lawsuit now that Carolyn was dead, it wasn't Liz's concern anymore. But...

'What about Mags's reputation?' she said. 'Everyone's avoiding the café because they think she poisoned Neil Grogan. Isn't it better to clear her name?'

Kevin grinned. 'Why don't you just admit it?'

'Admit what?'

'That you love the excitement. The thrill of trying to catch a murderer.'

Liz grinned back. He knew her too well. 'Will Anna be helping with the post-mortem? If so, she might want to keep an eye out for anything unusual.'

Kevin's face clouded. 'We've split up.'

'What? Why?'

'It just wasn't working out. We hardly ever saw each other, thanks to our shifts. And when we did, we were both too stressed to enjoy it.'

'I'm sorry to hear that.'

He stared bleakly out over the roiling waves of the North Sea. She guessed the break-up had been Anna's decision, and couldn't help but feel a motherly twinge of concern. She and Mark hadn't been able to have children – he'd had a bad dose of mumps as a teenager that had made him infertile. They'd talked about adopting, but decided not to. They both had fulfilling careers and each other, and that had been enough. Now he was dead, of course, she couldn't help wondering if they'd made the right decision. No one wanted to be alone. Her frustrated maternal urges surfaced occasionally, and she did her best to suppress them, but she couldn't deny she was very fond of Kevin. She resisted the urge to pat his hand.

'You never know,' she said, 'it might still work out.'

'Maybe.' He shrugged. 'In the meantime, there's always work.'

'But you know what they say – all work and no play...?'

He grinned. 'Pays the mortgage?'

She grinned back.

'Okay... so...' He emptied his cup. 'If Carolyn Grogan was murdered... IF she was murdered... who would want both her and her husband dead?'

Liz's phone rang.

'I've just had a call from our solicitor,' said Tilly. *'It's bad news. Philip Grogan's still pursuing the claim against Mags.'*

'What? That's awful.'

'I know. Oh, Liz, I don't know what to do!'

As KEVIN WENT BACK to the station, Liz headed to the Full Moon Café. There was no one there apart from Tilly doing a crossword at the counter. After the bustle of the town's Christmas streets, the emptiness of the café came as something of a shock.

'How is Mags?' asked Liz, perching on a stool.

'Not great. The news has really floored her. She's gone back to bed.'

Liz looked around. 'Where's Grazyna? Does she have the day off?'

'She's gone,' said Tilly.

'Gone?'

'She's found another job on the West Cliff. The Copper Kettle.'

Liz was astonished. It wasn't like Grazyna to abandon her friends in their hour of need. Tilly saw her expression.

'She didn't want to take it, but I made her. If she doesn't have a job when they review her immigration case, it will count against her, and I can't guarantee I can keep this place going much longer.' Tilly waved desolately around the café. 'Just look at it.'

In spite of the festive decorations and twinkling lights, it felt empty and joyless. The bell on the door tinkled as it opened. They both turned to see who it was.

Helen Grogan looked a little more rested and much less stressed than the last time they'd seen her.

'Hello,' she said. She joined them at the counter.

'Hi, Helen, can I get you anything?' asked Tilly.

'No, thank you.' Helen looked embarrassed. 'I'm just coming in to apologise. About Philip. I've tried to persuade him to drop the lawsuit, but he won't budge. He's not usually this... angry... but with everything that's happened the last couple of weeks...'

'Don't worry about it,' said Tilly. 'It's not your fault.'

'It's horribly ungrateful after everything you've done. I won't give up. I will keep trying to change his mind.'

'Thank you. But, like I said, don't worry about it.'

Helen nodded at them both. 'Merry Christmas.'

'Merry Christmas.'

'Merry Christmas.'

As Helen went out, she held the door open for Irwin. He looked dapper in a tweed overcoat, paisley muffler and flat cap.

'Brrrr.' He stamped his feet to warm them up. 'It's brass-monkey weather out there. I thought I'd come in for something to warm me up.'

'Bless you,' said Tilly, 'for swimming against the tide.' She splashed hot water from the urn into a teapot. Irwin scanned the empty café as he sat at the nearest table, then met Liz's eye. He raised his eyebrows in silent comment.

'Aren't you working today?' asked Liz.

'No, that's me finished for the holidays. I'm a man of leisure now for two whole weeks.'

Tilly put the teapot and a mug beside him. 'What can I get you to eat, Irwin?'

'A tuna melt toastie, please.'

'Coming right up.' Tilly headed through the beaded curtain into the kitchen. 'Do you want chips or crisps with it?' she called back.

'Crisps, please.'

When she'd gone, Irwin grimaced. 'Things still not going well here, I see.'

'Philip Grogan isn't going to drop the claim.'

'I imagine his father's funeral didn't put him in the best frame of mind.'

Liz looked at him. Was he talking about the funeral generally, or did he mean the singing fiasco?

'It was a bit of a disaster, wasn't it?'

'Just a bit,' she agreed.

'I've tried making subtle hints, but Mum's impervious. She loves singing so much. I can't tell her the truth. I can't tell her no one wants her there. She'd be devastated.'

'I can see you're in a difficult situation.'

Irwin stirred his tea. 'I've heard a rumour that Gregory's going to cancel our appearance at the Christmas Eve carol service.'

'I've heard that too.'

Irwin sighed. 'I'm completely out of ideas.'

Liz thought about it. 'What about hypnosis?'

Irwin shook his head. 'Doesn't work.'

'You've tried it?'

Irwin nodded. 'When I was a teenager. I was dreadfully embarrassed by her back then. Not so much these days – *"I have blushed so oft to acknowledge her that I am brazed to it".*'

'What did you do?' she asked.

'I made a tape.' He waggled his fingers at Liz, in imitation of a hypnotist. *'You do not need to speak so loudly. We will hear you anyway.* That kind of thing. I ran it on a loop on my old tape recorder in her bedroom when she was asleep.'

Liz's lips twitched at the thought of a young Irwin resorting to such desperate measures. 'No luck?'

'She slept right through it. If anything, the next day she was even louder.'

'I've often wondered why she doesn't always have a sore throat.'

Irwin sighed. 'After seven decades of shouting, her vocal cords are like leather.' He frowned and paused. His eyes widened as he looked at Liz. 'Unless—'

The café door burst open, startling them both. Detective Inspector Flint strode towards the table, every atom thrilling with triumph.

She slapped something down in front of Liz.

'Yours, I believe?'

It was Liz's lost glove.

15

W hitby police station was an unlovely seventies building on the outskirts of town, with absolutely no authority or redeeming features. Liz imagined it would be a depressing place to work, but reserved the right not to feel sorry for Detective Inspector Flint at that particular moment.

'You don't deny this is your glove?' snapped Flint, across the table of one of the interview rooms. It wasn't one Liz had been in before, and she'd been in quite a few.

'The other one's at home. Thanks for finding it for me. It does seem a bit of a song and dance just to return it though.'

'Song and dance?' Flint glanced at DC Williams, who was sitting to her left. He winced. Flint glared back at Liz. 'This is a serious investigation!'

'Into what?'

'You know perfectly well.'

Liz just looked at her.

'You were at the church the night Neil Grogan's body was stolen.'

'You know I was. You saw me there.'

Flint prodded the glove that lay on the table between them. 'You say you lost this. Lost it where?'

'If I'd known that, it wouldn't have been lost, would it?'

'Don't get clever. Where do you *think* you lost it?'

Liz shrugged. 'Could have been anywhere. In the town. Or up on the East Cliff. I walk my dog up there quite a lot. Where did you find it?'

Flint ignored the question. 'Where were you on Wednesday night?'

'I don't remember exactly. Why is that important?'

'Just answer the question.'

'Wednesday night.' Liz made a show of trying to think. 'I had a night in. And a bath.'

'You saw no one all night?'

'Just Nelson and my rubber duck.'

'Very convenient.'

'Why? Do I need an alibi?'

Flint picked up the glove. 'When the funeral directors came to collect Neil Grogan after he'd been returned, they found this. *Under* his body.' She paused for dramatic effect. 'Several people have identified it as yours.'

'I see.'

Flint gave her a look of satisfaction.

'I might have lost it in the church. Perhaps the thieves just put the body on top of it?'

Flint blinked. 'They saw it lying there, right in the middle of the nave, and just decided to put the body on top of it?'

'Yes.'

'That's your best explanation?'

'I can't *prove* they did, obviously.' The unspoken sequel to that statement was '*and you can't prove they didn't*'.

'Reverend Garraway saw three people running from the scene. I think one of them was you.'

'What does Gillian think?'

'If your friend *Gillian* did recognise you, she's hardly going to tell me, is she?'

Liz had to concede that point.

Flint stood up and turned to the constable. 'Okay, Williams, this is getting us nowhere. See her out.' She glared at Liz. 'For now. Don't think you've heard the last of this.'

Liz followed Williams out of the interview room, along the corridor towards the waiting area.

'It's okay,' said Liz. 'I know my way from here.'

Williams nodded and gave her a grim smile. He left her and retraced his steps as she headed out to the waiting room. Then something occurred to Liz, and she turned around again.

Flint and Williams were in the interview room together.

'Check CCTV on Church Street Wednesday night,' said Flint. 'She wasn't at home, and I'll prove it. I know she's lying to us.' Her eyes widened as she spotted Liz in the doorway.

'Erm... sorry to intrude. Can I have my glove back?'

Kevin caught up with Liz a few minutes later as she was leaving, without her glove but with a sizeable flea in her ear. He ran after her on the pavement outside.

'What's going on?' he gasped. 'I heard Flint had brought you in.' He glanced up to make sure they couldn't be seen from any of the station windows. 'What for? Was it Neil Grogan?'

Liz nodded.

'I warned you that she had you in the frame. But she must have found something, to bring you in?'

'My glove. It was in the church.'

'That doesn't sound too bad.' Kevin frowned. 'Am I missing something?'

'It was under Grogan's body when they found him.'

Kevin's eyes opened wide, then narrowed again. 'Please tell me—'

'I'm telling you nothing. What I don't tell you can't get you into trouble.'

His mouth snapped shut again. He wasn't pleased. 'Suit yourself. But that works both ways.'

'What do you mean?'

'I have a juicy piece of information I was going to give you, but I don't think I will now.'

'Oh.'

'What I don't tell you can't get you into trouble.'

Touche. Kevin's eyes gleamed with humour as they stared at each other. An impasse.

He spoke first. 'Full disclosure? *Quid pro quo*?'

Liz hesitated, then sighed and nodded. 'Full disclosure. But not here.'

Kevin looked at his watch. 'Your place? Forty-five minutes?'

YIP, yip!

Nelson was overjoyed to see her when she got home. He'd been on his own for four hours, much longer than she generally liked to leave him.

'No accidents? What a good boy!' She rubbed his ears enthusiastically.

She felt guilty, but it was hardly her fault that Flint had dragged her into the police station. It was a bit of a worry, though. If something had happened to her, what would have happened to Nelson? No one else had a key to Gull Cottage. She made a mental note to do something about that.

She took Nelson for a quick pee break on the shore.

When they got back, she just had enough time to freshen up and put the kettle on before she heard Kevin's knock at the door.

'It's open.'

It wasn't Kevin.

'You should not leave your door open like this. You are too trusting.'

'Lovely to see you, Grazyna. Cup of tea? I've just put the kettle on.'

'Thank you, no. I was passing on my way to the smoke-house for kippers, for the boys, and thought I would see if you were in. I wanted a fast word.'

'Okay.'

Grazyna hesitated. For a fast word, she seemed quite reluctant to begin. 'I do not want you to think ill of me. For taking a new job. I cannot afford to look bad at my hearing. I need to be in full-time employment.'

'I know that. We all know that.'

'I still think of you and Tilly and Mags as my friends.'

'I should hope so!'

Grazyna nodded. 'You will come up to the Copper Kettle to see me, yes?'

'Of course.'

It seemed to Liz that Grazyna looked a little happier as she left. Kevin turned up a couple of minutes later. He sipped his tea and listened, open-mouthed, as Liz related her adventures with Neil Grogan's corpse.

'You think Gillian recognised you?'

'I think she might have.'

'If she was going to say anything to Flint, she'd have said it by now.'

'I suppose.' Liz was slightly reassured. 'I told Flint I was home all night, but she's having CCTV checked. She might spot me and Tilly getting picked up by Helen. And then they'll be in trouble too.'

'I wouldn't worry about it. She would have to know exactly which cameras to check, at exactly what time. We don't have the manpower to spend hours going through CCTV.'

'Good.' Liz was relieved. 'So that's my *quid*. What's your *quo*?'

'What?'

'What were you going to tell me?'

'Oh, yes. Anna called me this afternoon.'

'That's nice.' Liz searched his face, but there was no trace of a smile. 'Isn't it?'

'She assisted at Carolyn Grogan's autopsy this morning.'

'Oh.' Liz realised she'd been barking up the wrong tree. 'And?'

'She died of a heart attack. But... they found a puncture wound on her neck. Into a carotid artery. Very easy to miss, but they caught it.'

'Wow.'

'They're still waiting for the tox report, but they do expect it to show something.'

'That would put Neil Grogan's death in a very different light, wouldn't it? Do you think they'll exhume his body?'

'It's possible. Poor Grogan. He might be dead, but he's really having a rough time of it.' He drained his mug. 'Got to dash.' He winked. 'Flint probably has some CCTV she wants me to go through.'

When he'd gone, she washed up their dirty mugs thoughtfully. Who could have wanted to kill Carolyn Grogan? The obvious answer was Neil's children, but it didn't necessarily follow that Philip, Adam and Helen would inherit Neil's original estate now that Carolyn was dead. Carolyn might have family of her own who would claim it. There was something not adding up somewhere. Something she couldn't see. Perhaps she'd been looking too closely at the family for likely suspects, and should spread her net wider? Who else might have an axe to grind with the Grogans?

16

The next day was Sunday, so Liz knew that Mike Howson wouldn't be making his usual deliveries to the smokehouse next door. She also knew that he and his wife were regulars at St Mary's, so she waited for the church bells to clang on the clifftop above the cottage before leaving for her morning walk with Nelson. By this happy mixture of contrivance and good luck, she arrived at the bottom of the abbey steps just as Mike and his wife appeared at the end of Church Street.

'Mrs Mac! Good morning to you!' Mike leaned down to scratch Nelson's ears.

'Morning.' Liz also nodded a greeting to Mike's wife, a capable-looking woman in a Barbour jacket. She didn't know her first name, but had often bought haddock from her in the shop on Baxtergate.

'You going up to the church?' asked Mike.

'Just the churchyard. Nelson loves it up there.'

'Rabbits, eh?' Mike winked at the bull terrier. Nelson ignored him.

They all climbed together.

As Liz expected, she didn't have to broach the subject of the Grogans herself.

'A little bird tells me they might be going to dig Neil Grogan up again.'

'Oh?' Liz pretended that was news. Mike really did have eyes and ears everywhere. 'Poor man.'

He gave her a sideways look. 'If you say so. There were a lot of folk didn't much care for him.'

'Really?' Liz prompted.

'He was elected mayor, right enough – people trusted him to get stuff done, but on a personal level it was a different story.'

'Any particular reason?' asked Liz.

'He was a hard businessman. Tough. Had many run-ins with people over the years.'

'Anyone in particular you can think of?'

'Funny you should ask that, because one of them's just up ahead of us there.' Mike nodded up the steps. Liz looked. There were quite a few people making their way up to the church in front of them.

'Who?' she asked.

'Dora Spackle.'

Nelson growled. He knew the name of his nemesis, something that had caused much amusement when Liz and her young friend Niall had discovered it in the summer. Sure enough, Liz could see the figure of the museum curator stamping up the last few steps at the clifftop. She hoped Nelson wouldn't spot her too.

Mike continued, puffing as he climbed. 'She had a run-in with Grogan a few years back. Pretty spectacular. It was in the paper and everything. I can't remember the exact details... the whys and wherefores... but she smashed the window of that shop of his. She'd had a few too many, as I recall.'

Liz was astonished. Dora Spackle? Drunk? It seemed unlikely, but Mike was generally a reliable gossip.

They parted company at the top of the steps, and Mike and his wife headed into the church while Liz and Nelson went into the churchyard. As soon as she unclipped him from his lead, Nelson charged into the long grass between the gravestones. His head was so large compared to his body that Liz always marvelled he could run at all without toppling forward onto his nose. He'd never managed to catch a rabbit, and she doubted he ever would.

She did a couple of laps of the church while he did his best to prove her wrong. Walking anticlockwise around a church – *widdershins about a kirk* – was supposed to be bad luck in Scotland. But she wasn't in Scotland anymore and wasn't superstitious either. *Widdershins* was the way she preferred to do it.

After twenty minutes or so she called Nelson back to her. He returned, rabbitless and reluctant.

'Never mind,' she said, clipping him back onto his lead. 'Better luck next time.' She was keen to head back before the churchgoers came out. A splash of water fell on her cheek. She lifted her face to the sky, which had darkened a lot since she'd left her cottage. She got to the top of the abbey steps before it started to rain, a hard downpour that stung her face and soaked through her coat in a matter of minutes. She hurried Nelson down the steps. By the time they got back to Gull Cottage, they were both wet to the skin. She towelled Nelson dry, then stripped down to her underwear and headed upstairs for a shower.

She'd just got out, and was brushing her wet hair, when she heard a knock at the door downstairs.

Yip, yip, yip.

'Hang on! I'm coming,' she called, more to the dog than to whoever was knocking, who probably couldn't hear her anyway. She wrapped herself hastily in a towel and hurried down the twisting staircase as fast as she could without breaking her neck or flashing the dog. She opened the door.

'Benedict!'

He had rain dripping off his hair and running down his face. She ushered him inside. His gaze widened as he took in her wet hair and state of undress. 'Sorry if I disturbed you. I didn't get you out of the shower, did I?' Was it her imagination, or did he actually blush?

'No, I'd just finished.' She tucked the towel more firmly around her. 'Come in out of the rain.' She ushered him into the kitchen.

'I've just been to the service at St Mary's,' he continued, 'and bumped into Gregory. He's cancelled this afternoon's practice. I told him I would come and let you know, as I was passing. Save him a phone call.'

Henrietta Street was hardly on Benedict's way home to Pannet Park. He'd come out of his way, and in the rain too. Liz tried not to think about the possible implications of that and turned her mind to other things. It wasn't a good sign that Gregory had cancelled practice.

'Do you think he's going to pull out of the carol service?'

'I wouldn't be surprised.'

Drip, drip.

A splash of water fell onto the kitchen table beside them, darkening the unpolished pine. They both looked up. There was a stain on the ceiling. Another droplet of water gathered there, trembled, and fell onto the table.

Drip.

'Oh,' said Liz.

'Looks like you have a leak.'

Her first thought was that she'd left the shower running, and the drain had somehow blocked. But she swiftly revised that theory – the shower wasn't directly above them, and she was pretty sure she'd turned it off. Then she landed on the likeliest culprit. The roof!

The next droplet trembled on the ceiling above them. Instinctively, Liz pushed a dirty mug underneath it.

'I have some tiles missing,' she said to Benedict. 'I tried to get someone out to fix them, but...'

'Must be pretty bad, if water's come through all the way down here. Would you like me to take a look?'

'What do you know about roofs?' That came out snippier than she had intended. She tried to soften it with a smile, but it felt more like a grimace.

'A bit. I do my own repairs when I can.'

'It's pouring with rain.'

'Well... yes.' To her relief he refrained from stating the obvious – the roof wouldn't be leaking otherwise. He grinned. 'I'm soaked through anyway. I might as well take a look.'

'As long as you don't mind.' She didn't generally enjoy playing the helpless female, but she knew nothing about roofs and didn't want to spend Christmas afloat. 'I have spare tiles and roofing nails somewhere. I'll see if I can dig them out.'

'Erm...' Benedict hesitated. 'Maybe you should put some clothes on first?'

'CAN YOU SEE ANYTHING?'

'You were right.' Benedict's words were almost drowned out by the sound of the rain drumming on the roof. He had his head and most of his torso out of the roof window. 'There's a couple missing.'

He pulled his head back in again. 'And one that's broken, I think. I'll have to replace it.'

'Can you reach it from there?'

'No. I'll need to climb out.'

Liz grimaced. 'It's still pouring down. Perhaps it would be better to come back when it's stopped?'

'You could be flooded by then. Besides, I couldn't get any wetter.'

'But it's slippery.'

'I'll be fine, as long as you pass stuff out to me.'

Liz looked at him. She really didn't like the idea of him risking his neck out there. 'I can put buckets under it until the roofer gets here.'

Benedict stared down at her from his perch on the stepladder. 'All through Christmas? Don't be daft. I really don't mind. Honestly.'

Liz looked for his tell, the twitch of his lip that always betrayed him when he was lying. It wasn't there. She capitulated.

'Okay. As long as you're careful.'

Benedict grinned. 'I'll need a hammer and something to lever the damaged tile off. Let's have a look at your toolbox.'

It took almost an hour. By the time Benedict had replaced the smashed tile and restored the missing ones, he was soaked to the skin, and his teeth were chattering. Liz wasn't much better. She'd had her head out the window for most of it. Her hair felt as if it were frozen, and her ears were completely numb.

Benedict closed the window with a thump and gave a groan of relief.

'That should be fine now. But keep an eye on it.'

'I don't know how to thank you.'

'A cup of coffee would be good. And a shower, if that's okay?'

Liz didn't have any dry clothes that would fit him, so after he'd showered, he sat in the kitchen with a towel wrapped round his hips while his clothes steamed on the radiators. He sipped at his mug of coffee.

'Not the most relaxing way to spend a Sunday afternoon,' said Liz.

'Oh. I've had worse. And wetter, believe it or not.'

She did. He never said much about his years in the Navy, but she knew he'd seen active service. It wasn't something she felt she could ask him about.

'Are you sure you don't want something in that coffee to warm you up?'

'Tempting, but no. I don't want you to have to roll me home like a barrel. Not a good way to spend a Sunday either.'

His words reminded Liz about something.

'How well do you know Dora Spackle?'

'Dora?' He pulled a puzzled face at her abrupt change of subject. 'Pretty well, I suppose. We both move in museum circles.'

'Do you know if she has a drink problem?'

His eyes opened wide. 'Not that I know of. But, there again, it isn't something she would probably broadcast, is it? What on earth makes you ask?'

'She had a run-in with Neil Grogan, apparently. A few years ago. Mike Howson said she was drunk.'

Benedict furrowed his brow. 'Now that you mention it, that does ring a bell. When was it, exactly?'

'I'm not sure.'

Benedict shook his head. 'Like I said, it rings a bell, but I don't remember any details. But surely you don't think Dora killed him?'

'No.' She had to admit, that was far-fetched. 'I'm just doing some general digging. Philip Grogan still wants to sue Mags for his father's death. The café's really suffering.' She was being a little disingenuous. If the coroner decided that Carolyn Grogan's death was also suspicious, the police would exhume Neil, and Mags would probably be off the hook. But Liz was still curious. Kevin had been bang on the money when he'd said she enjoyed investigating murders. She seemed to have acquired a taste for it since coming to Whitby.

Benedict had been watching her face closely. She looked up and caught him. He looked away.

'I should be going,' he said, and drained his coffee.

'Your clothes aren't dry yet.'

'They'll do. Warm and wet is a lot better than cold and wet. I'll be home in two shakes.'

17

When Benedict had gone, Liz put her tools and stepladder away and mopped the floor of the attic room. She was incredibly grateful that Benedict had fixed the roof, but the whole episode had unsettled her. She'd always thought that Benedict was completely oblivious to her as a woman, but now she wasn't quite so sure. He'd been giving off strange vibes ever since that odd moment in his office when he'd picked the gravel out of her palms. He'd come out of his way in the pouring rain to tell her that the choir had been cancelled, and then taken immense trouble with her roof. He'd actually blushed when he'd caught her wearing only a towel. But the main thing that had made her wonder was the way he'd just looked at her in the kitchen. It was... odd. But did it mean anything? She was so out of the loop when it came to sex and romance – it had been thirty years since she'd met and married Mark, and there hadn't been anyone since – she didn't trust her own instincts at all. She was also pretty sure that Benedict still held a torch for Gillian Garraway, and the last thing she wanted was to be a rebound. She'd rather have nothing than that.

But even if that wasn't the case, even if Benedict *was* interested in her that way, was she really ready to start a brand-new relationship? Could she even be bothered? She'd spent five years on her own, with nobody but herself and, latterly, Nelson to think about. Did she really want to start having to navigate the needs and feelings of someone else? She sighed and put her mop and bucket away. She didn't know the answer to that and probably wouldn't until... if... the actual moment came when she needed to decide.

THE NEXT DAY, Liz was up and about as the sun rose. The rain had gone, and the exit of the clouds had brought a significant drop in temperature. Water had turned to ice, treacherous underfoot as Liz and Nelson headed up to the graveyard. She shoved her hands deeper into her pockets – Inspector Flint still had one of her gloves, and she hadn't had the chance to buy new ones.

Because the ground was so icy, they went up the donkey path to the abbey, rather than climbing the steps. The donkey path was a steep, cobbled lane that ran beside the steps on a lower level. On a busy day, you could look up and see the heads of people on the steps above and hear them chatter as they went up and down. That morning there was no one else out and about, so Liz and Nelson had the donkey path and the graveyard to themselves.

Afterwards, she settled Nelson in his basket and headed straight out again. She had to buy herself another pair of gloves, but first there was something she needed to do.

The offices of the *Whitby Bugle* were on Flowergate, above the Yorkshire Rose Building Society. Not so very long ago the premises of a newspaper would have been filled with the clatter of printing presses and the smell of ink. But now, in the digital age, it was much the same as any other open-plan office, with phones ringing and people milling around. It reminded Liz a bit of the police station.

A young woman spotted her standing at the reception desk and came over to see what she wanted.

'I'd like to look through your archives, please.'

'There's a fee. Fifteen pounds.'

Liz handed over the money.

'What kind of timeline will you be looking at?' asked the woman. 'After two thousand, everything's on the system, but before that it's on microfiche.'

'Post two thousand.' She certainly hoped so. Mike and Benedict had both been vague about the date of Dora's attack on Neil Grogan's shop, which made her think it must have been quite a while ago. It certainly hadn't happened since she had come to Whitby, or she would have heard about it. She hoped she wouldn't have to go back twenty years.

The woman led her to a workstation surrounded by screens, where there was a computer and a pad for taking notes. She logged Liz into the system and showed her how to use the search engine.

'I'll leave you to it.'

The ancient computer had never been state of the art even when it was new, but whoever had entered the records on the system had done a pretty good job. Information could be retrieved several different ways – by subject, date or keyword – and showed not only the articles themselves, but a PDF of the page they'd originally appeared on in the newspaper. Liz found Dora straight away. The most recent results dated from the previous summer, covering the theft of the medieval relic St Ælfflaed's girdle from the museum and the subsequent review of the security systems. Before that, in two thousand and eighteen, there were a couple of articles about

Dora's appointment as head curator. Then there was a size-able gap until two thousand and nine.

'Bingo.'

Woman charged with criminal damage due to appear in court

Dora Hildegard Spackle is alleged to have damaged a shop window worth £485 at the premises belonging to Neil Grogan in Baxtergate, Whitby, on March 14th.
She is also charged with disorderly conduct and drunken behaviour.
The 50-year-old, of New Way Ghaut, Whitby, is due to appear in North Yorkshire Magistrates' Court today.

The article was dated August 7. Liz scanned ahead but couldn't find anything about the court appearance itself or the results. Presumably Dora had been fined, but if so, there was nothing about it in the *Bugle*. Frustrated, Liz typed March 14, 2009, into the search engine. There was nothing there about the vandalism, but Liz found something a couple of days later, on March 16.

Police are looking to identify a woman captured on CCTV in connection with criminal damage to a shop in Baxtergate, Whitby.
The damage occurred between 10.20pm and 10.40pm on Saturday, March 14.
North Yorkshire Police have today released a CCTV image of the woman they want to speak to in connection with the incident.
The force calls on anyone with any information about the woman pictured or the disturbance in Baxtergate to come forward.

You can contact the independent charity CrimeWatchers anonymously on 0800 777 222. No personal details are taken, information cannot be traced or recorded, and you will not go to court or have to speak to police when contacting CrimeWatchers.

There were two photographs in the article, one of the boarded-up shop, and one of the suspect taken from CCTV footage. The suspect was quite small, but was wielding what seemed to be a broom shank with the verve of a ju-jitsu master. The photo had caught the moment the glass was beginning to crack. It must have taken a few whacks to do it. Liz peered more closely at the photo. The grainy image gave quite a good view of the twisted features beneath the cloche hat. Liz was astonished the police had had to put out an appeal – almost everyone in the town must have recognised Dora. She imagined the CrimeWatchers' line would have been ringing off the hook.

It was all very interesting and – if she was honest – not a little amusing, but still gave no clue as to what had made Dora stoop to such extreme measures in the first place. Dora wasn't a woman easily swayed by emotion. The previous article about the court appearance had also said she'd been drunk and disorderly. That seemed out of character too.

Liz was about to log off the computer when another article on the same page caught her eye.

Star pupils awarded science prize.

It was the photograph rather than the article that attracted her attention – five sixth-formers beamed at the camera, dressed in the distinctive school uniform of Whitby Academy. Liz recognised the girl in the centre, who was holding the ugly glass award aloft in one hand. Carolyn

Grogan's shiny hair was pulled into a ponytail, and she had a broad grin on her face. A girl who thought she had her whole life ahead of her. Liz felt a twinge of guilt at her previous amusement.

There was no doubt in Liz's mind that Carolyn had been murdered. It was simply too much of a coincidence that she and Neil had both dropped dead within a fortnight of each other. The question was why were they killed? Money wasn't likely to be a motive – Carolyn's relatives would inherit Neil's estate. It had to be personal.

Liz thought she knew Dora Spackle well enough to be pretty sure she wasn't a murderer. But there had to be a reason Dora had put herself so spectacularly on the wrong side of the law. If Liz could find out how Neil had provoked her, she might find a clue to the killer's motives too. It was a long shot, but one worth taking.

On her way home, Liz bought herself some new gloves, a black leather pair with a thermal lining. They weren't as nice as the pair she'd sacrificed to the North Yorkshire PD, but at least they would keep her hands warm. She also stopped off at her favourite baker on Church Street and bought a delicious-looking festive stollen with cherries and marzipan. The smell of it made her mouth water.

She had intended to go straight home after that, to formulate a proper plan on how to tackle Dora, but as she was about to walk past the concealed entrance to New Way Ghaut, she hesitated. New Way Ghaut was a narrow, overcrowded lane that ran between Church Street and the shore, its entrance an unlikely stone tunnel protected by an iron gate. It looked more like someone's backyard than the main entrance to more than a dozen cottages. On impulse, Liz opened the gate and ducked into the tunnel. There was no time like the present.

She knew that Dora lived in Anchor Cottage, but had no idea where on New Way Ghaut she would find it. She peered at the nameplate of every cottage as she passed until she was almost at the end of the passage, where it led back up onto Church Street. There she found Anchor Cottage, down a narrow path to her left, huddled underneath a red-brick extension of the Board Inn, which fronted on Church Street. Unlike the other cottages on the Ghaut, which were all eighteenth century, Anchor Cottage was a nineteen seventies building made of red brick, with a plain door and no decorative touches. A strange choice for a history buff. Liz marched up the path, took a deep breath and knocked on the door.

No one answered.

Liz realised that Dora was probably at work. Not everyone had finished for the Christmas holidays as early as Irwin. She turned away from the door with a mixture of disappointment and relief. As she was about to rejoin the main path, she found her way blocked by a solid figure carrying two overloaded supermarket carrier bags. She and Dora stared at each other in surprise.

'I've just been to your cottage,' stammered Liz.

Dora scowled. 'What for?'

Liz lifted the bakery box. 'To make a peace offering.'

'Why?'

'Because it's Christmas.'

Dora eyed the box. 'There's no point trying to bribe me. I don't like cake.' She shouldered her way past Liz. Liz was at a bit of a loss. Should she just leave, or persist? Luckily, Fate intervened.

As Dora fumbled in her pocket for her key, the seam on one of the carrier bags split, dumping its contents on the ground. Tins rolled everywhere.

'Bugger.'

Liz placed her cake box on a nearby plant pot and hurried to gather up Dora's purchases. As well as the tins, they included a bar of chocolate, a single-sized Christmas pudding, and a frozen turkey meal for one. Liz felt a wave of compassion. She'd been invited to Christmas dinner by Mags and Tilly. Under the current circumstances, it wasn't likely to be the jolliest gathering, but at least she wouldn't have to eat alone. She tried to keep the pity off her face as she stood up. But Dora had disappeared inside the cottage, leaving the door open. Liz ventured inside.

'Where shall I put these?' she asked Dora, who had dumped her own bag on the kitchen floor.

'Anywhere.'

Liz put her armful of groceries on the table.

'There's still a couple of things outside,' she said. 'I'll go and get them.'

She hurried out to retrieve the final items and the cake box she'd left on the plant pot. When she came back inside, Dora was taking her coat off.

'I suppose you'll want a cup of tea now,' she said begrudgingly.

Liz was surprised. She'd expected Dora to send her packing straight away.

'That would be nice, thank you.'

Dora put the kettle on and indicated that Liz should sit down.

'Take your coat off.'

Liz did as she was told and hung her coat on the back of the door while Dora busied herself with the teapot and caddy. Liz supposed she shouldn't be surprised that Dora made tea the traditional way, with leaves and a strainer. She looked around surreptitiously. The kitchen seemed to have been frozen in the nineteen seventies, with orange melamine units and brown everything else – brown lino, brown wall tiles, brown wallpaper, and ugly brown crockery on the shelves.

Liz wondered whether to broach the subject of Nelson, but decided not to, at least not just yet. That wasn't why she was there. Dora put some of the groceries on the table into the fridge.

'Good job there were no bottles of booze in that bag,' Liz said.

'I don't drink,' muttered Dora. 'Not anymore.'

'Not since your run-in with Neil Grogan's shop window?'

Dora stared at Liz.

Liz stared back, fronting it out. The change of subject hadn't been very elegant, or diplomatic, but was as good a way to accomplish her mission as any.

Dora snapped her mouth shut and turned away so Liz couldn't see her face. 'You are very rude.'

Liz gave a bark of laughter. 'You wouldn't win any prizes for tact yourself, Dora.'

To Liz's surprise, when Dora turned back to put the teapot on the table, she didn't seem to be angry.

'Then I suppose we're well matched, aren't we?' she said as she poured. 'Two unpleasant old ladies having tea together.' She saw Liz's offended expression and smiled. Actually smiled. Liz couldn't have been more surprised if she'd leapt onto the table and done the cancan.

'Milk?' Dora's smile had gone, but her air of amusement remained.

'Yes, please.'

'Peace offering, my backside. You want to know what happened between me and Grogan.'

'I do.' There was no point denying it.

'Why? Do you think someone killed him?'

'Maybe.'

'And you think it was me?'

'No.'

Dora raised her eyebrows and gave Liz a searching look.

'No, I don't. I'm just trying to get a picture of the kind of man he was.'

'He was a shark, that's what he was.'

'Will you tell me about it?'

Dora sighed.

Liz pressed her advantage. 'If you've never told anyone your side of the story, it might be good to get it off your chest?'

'I suppose it couldn't do any harm. Even if it's you.' She settled herself at the table and took a slurp of tea. 'Are your parents still alive?'

Liz was surprised by the question. 'No. Why do you ask?'

'Mine neither. My mother died February two thousand and nine.'

Just before the window incident.

'She'd never been an easy woman to get on with, and after my father died, she didn't get any easier. But even so...' Dora shrugged. 'She was all I had, and she had a hard death. I didn't take it well. She didn't leave a lot, just this cottage and a few bits and bobs. Ornaments. Jewellery. None of it worth very much except...' She broke off and went out of the room.

She returned a few moments later with a Victorian photograph in a silver frame, which she gave to Liz. It was a studio portrait of a very upright and surprisingly beautiful woman with ringlets, in a high-necked gown.

'My grandmother. Wearing her favourite necklace.'

Liz peered more closely at the photo.

'Whitby Jet,' said Liz. It was a substantial piece, with a finely carved cameo pendant depicting what looked to be an arrangement of seashells and lilies.

Dora nodded. 'She was widowed at a young age and wore

that mourning locket for the rest of her life. I should never...'
She broke off again and gazed bleakly into her teacup. When
she looked back at Liz, her eyes were defiant. 'The long and
the short of it was I needed the money for the funeral. I took
it to Neil Grogan.'

Liz could guess where this was going.

'He offered me seventy pounds, and I took it. I knew it
wasn't anywhere near what it was worth, but I took it. And I
regretted it almost straight away. I went back the next day and
asked him... begged him to sell it back to me.'

'He wouldn't?'

Dora gave a bitter snort of laughter. 'I went to Deborah,
who I've known for years. She tried to reason with him, to
persuade him to sell it back to me... to *give* it back to me... but
he wouldn't. He stood there and told us both that I'd made a
fair bargain. He wouldn't budge.' Dora fell silent.

'So...?'

'So I spent the rest of the day drinking, and went back to
the shop with a broom.'

'Did you have any run-ins with him after that?'

Dora shook her head. 'I steered well clear. But I can't say I
was sorry to hear he was dead.' She saw the shock on Liz's
face, and her smile returned. It had a hard edge. 'Aren't you
going to open that cake of yours?'

Liz pulled the box towards her on the table and opened it.
Dora's nose wrinkled.

'What?' said Liz.

'Marzipan.' Dora sniffed. 'I hate marzipan.'

18

L iz ate most of the cake herself when she got back to Gull Cottage. Dora's tale hadn't been particularly illuminating other than highlighting what a nasty piece of work Neil Grogan had been. To take advantage of a grieving woman like that was callous in the extreme, but perhaps that kind of transaction wasn't unusual for him? Mike Howson had said he wasn't well liked. How many other people had he taken advantage of over the years? And of course, he wasn't just a jeweller, he'd been involved with the council and racehorses too. She imagined those worlds could be just as cut-throat as the jewellery business, if not more so. Liz sighed. It was beginning to look as if there could be a lot of people who wanted Neil Grogan dead.

She dusted the crumbs off her chest and looked at Nelson, who was pretending not to be disappointed. She'd never fed him from the table, but it didn't stop him living in hope.

'Cake's not good for dogs,' she said. 'Too much sugar.'

It wasn't good for middle-aged women either, but Liz pushed that thought away. It was replaced by another – there was someone else who would know all Grogan's dark secrets. She should talk to her again.

SHE WENT to the café first. It had been a couple of days since she'd seen Tilly and Mags, and she didn't want them to think she'd forgotten about them or their troubles. To her surprise Lukasz and Eryk were there, busy with wrapping paper and ribbon at one of the tables.

'Schools finished for the holidays,' said Tilly by way of explanation, 'but the Copper Kettle isn't keen on having them there. I said Grazyna could leave them with me. It's not as if I have a lot else going on.'

Apart from the boys, there was no one else in the café, but Tilly looked resigned rather than desperate.

'I hear Flint took you in for questioning,' she said to Liz. 'Did Gillian recognise you?'

'I don't think so.' Liz shook her head. 'Or if she did, she didn't tell Flint. Remember I lost my glove? They found it under Grogan's body.'

'Shit.' Tilly pulled a face. 'How did you wriggle out of that?'

'I didn't. I just told Flint I must have dropped it in the church, and the body thieves must have put Grogan on top of it. I can't prove that's what happened, but she can't prove it wasn't, either, so it's a stalemate.'

'For now.'

'For now,' agreed Liz. 'You might want to watch your step. If Flint thinks I'm involved, she won't have to look too far for an accomplice.'

'I'm surprised she hasn't pulled me in already.' Tilly looked thoughtful, then shrugged. 'It's nothing I couldn't handle. Can I get you anything to eat?'

Liz almost groaned. Her stomach was still full of stollen sponge, cherries and marzipan.

Tilly saw her expression and sighed. 'Don't worry about it. The price of a scone is hardly going to save us from bankruptcy.'

'Are things that bad?'

'Could be. If business doesn't pick up soon, we don't have much of a safety net.'

Liz was thoughtful. 'Have you seen Kevin lately?'

'Not for a few days. Why?'

Liz dropped her voice so the boys couldn't hear. 'It's possible Carolyn Grogan's death was suspicious.'

Tilly's eyes widened. 'But that means...'

Liz nodded. 'Neil Grogan might also have been murdered, and wasn't killed by his allergy. They might dig him up.'

Tilly slumped into a chair. 'That's the best news I've had for ages. I wonder why Kev hasn't mentioned it.' She scowled. 'He could have picked up the phone.'

'Perhaps he doesn't want to get your hopes up?'

'When will they know for sure?'

'They're waiting for blood results,' said Liz. 'Are you going to tell Mags?'

'I don't think so. Not yet. I don't think she could take another disappointment.'

'Probably wise.'

'Aren't you going to take your coat off?'

Liz stood up. 'I have to get on. Things to do, people to see.'

'You're still on for Christmas dinner?'

'Course! I'll see you before then, though, won't I? Are you coming to the service on Christmas Eve?' She knew Tilly and Mags weren't churchgoers, but thought they might make an exception for carols.

'Are you singing?'

'I hope so.'

Tilly frowned. 'There's some doubt about it?'

'Let's just say Gregory's having HR issues.'

'Oh. Well, fingers crossed. Yeah, sure, as long as you're singing, we'll be there.'

Liz headed for the door, but stopped again as she remembered something she'd wanted to ask.

'Would you keep a set of keys for me here? When Flint dragged me into the station, I realised that Nelson could have been left high and dry.'

'Course. No worries.'

'Thanks. I'll get a spare set cut now before I forget about it.'

SHE CROSSED the river and dropped her keys at the locksmith on Baxtergate before heading back over to Church Street and the Museum of Whitby Jet. There were only five shopping days left before Christmas. Many people had finished work, and the schools were out too. The streets were full of harassed parents herding their overexcited offspring from shop to shop. Liz couldn't help but overhear some of the exchanges.

'But Nana loves vodka. Why can't we get her some?'

'On a scale of one to ten, what are the chances of Santa bringing me a sloth?'

Liz grinned. She loved Christmas, even if it could be a lonely time of year for her personally. So many memories. She gave herself a shake as she arrived at the museum. The narrow entryway was crowded with people coming in and out and looking at the jewellery in the wall-mounted display cases. Liz shouldered her way through to the shop.

The shop wasn't quite so busy. A shop assistant in her twenties was putting together a pile of gift boxes, while

Deborah was serving two teenage girls, who were poring over the jewellery in the glass counter.

'I think those ones are just as nice,' said Deborah. 'More discreet. And they're a little bit cheaper.'

Deborah spotted Liz over the top of their heads and winked.

'Perfect. We'll take those, please,' said one of the girls. 'They're lovely.'

The girls settled on the pair that Deborah had recommended. Deborah wrapped them and put the transaction through the till. When the girls had gone, Deborah stepped out from behind the counter and joined Liz.

'Just in time,' she said. 'I'm gagging for a coffee. Can you manage here for twenty minutes, Leah?'

'Of course, Mrs Grogan.'

They went to the café directly opposite the museum. It was busy, but they managed to find a seat in a corner.

'Phew,' said Deborah. 'My feet are killing me.'

They ordered coffee, and Liz watched while Deborah devoured a filled baguette. She was still too full of cake to think about eating.

'Any plans for Christmas?' she asked.

'This year's going to be a bit different to what we planned. Neil and I used to take turns having the kids for Christmas dinner. It was supposed to be Neil's turn... not that they particularly liked spending time with Carolyn.' Deborah paused. 'We shouldn't have given her such a hard time.'

'Only natural, under the circumstances?'

Deborah shook her head. 'My marriage was over long before Carolyn came on the scene. It wasn't her fault, but we all blamed her. She had no family of her own. We could have made it so much easier for everyone.' Deborah shrugged. 'I suppose there's nothing we can do about it now.'

Liz was silent, thinking. If Carolyn had no family, that

meant that Adam, Philip and Helen would each inherit a third of his estate. Perhaps money *was* the motive. Liz sighed. With every two steps she took forward in the investigation, she seemed to take one step back.

'What about you?' Deborah's question snapped Liz back to the real world.

'Sorry?'

'Do you have plans for Christmas?'

'I'm going to friends' for dinner,' said Liz.

'That's nice. It's good not to spend Christmas on your own.'

Liz thought back to Dora's sad turkey dinner for one. 'I was talking to a friend of yours this morning. Dora Spackle.'

'How is Dora?' asked Deborah. 'I haven't spoken to her in a while.'

'Pretty much the same as usual. She mentioned you. She said you've known each other for years.'

Deborah nodded and wiped her mouth. 'We were at school together.'

'She told me about that business with the necklace.'

Deborah's eyes met Liz's. She sighed and crumpled her serviette onto her plate. 'That was awful. Really awful. I tried to help, but...'

'You couldn't persuade Neil to sell her the necklace back.'

'I told him he should *give* it back to her. He had no right taking advantage of her like that. But it was like talking to a brick wall. Neil could be... stubborn.'

Liz thought about Philip's refusal to drop the case against Mags. That apple hadn't fallen far from the tree.

'I'd better get back to the shop,' said Deborah. 'Leah will be struggling on her own.'

They paid the bill and put their coats on.

'Are you coming to choir tonight?' asked Liz.

'Is it definitely on? I'm surprised Gregory hasn't cancelled it. That woman.' She shook her head, then saw Liz's expression. 'Sorry. She's a friend of yours.'

'She is. But that doesn't make me deaf.' Liz sighed. 'Singing is supposed to be fun. It would be such a shame to cancel the carols, when everyone's practised so hard.'

'I suppose,' said Deborah. 'But a church is supposed to be a place of worship, not a music hall.'

19

'MY OLD MAN SAID FOLLOW THE VAN...' Iris broke off singing, and winked at Gregory, who had arrived late and was taking his coat off. 'JUST WARMING UP, GREG.'

'That's good.' He gave her a bleak look. 'Very good.'

Everyone else was already in their places. There was none of the usual chatter or gossip, not even any mention of Carolyn's recent death. Deborah took her seat at the piano while Gregory stepped up to his music stand with the air of a prisoner going to his own execution. He shuffled distractedly through his music.

'Shall we start with "Hark the Herald"?' suggested Deborah.

Gregory found the music. 'I suppose we might as well.'

Three-quarters of an hour later, everyone was more than ready for a tea break. Gillian handed out biscuits while everyone helped themselves to tea and coffee.

'DON'T YOU HAVE ANY WITH JAM IN? I DO LIKE A BIT OF JAM ON A MONDAY.'

'Sorry, Iris,' said Gillian. 'We only have digestives today.'

'I SUPPOSE THAT WILL DO.' Iris took a digestive and bit into it with gusto.

'Biscuit, Benedict?' said Gillian.

'Thanks.' He took one without making eye contact with Gillian, but Gillian's and Liz's eyes met briefly. Liz was shocked to see the pain there. Even if Benedict was over Gillian, Gillian clearly wasn't over him. That made Liz's position even more impossible.

Liz's bleak thoughts were interrupted by a loud intake of breath from Iris. Her biscuit had gone down the wrong way. She gagged and tried to catch her breath, but couldn't. Everyone looked at her. Her face crumpled in panic, and she thumped her own chest. But she still couldn't catch her breath. She bent over, face darkening. Everyone looked at each other, alarmed.

'Mum? Are you alright?' Irwin hurried to his mother and bent over her. 'She's choking!'

Liz realised she had to act fast. She grabbed Iris from behind and wrapped her arms around her abdomen. Then she heaved.

Once.

Twice.

Three times.

The offending piece of biscuit shot out of Iris's mouth and landed with a plop several yards away. Iris took a deep, shuddering breath.

'I'M ALRIGHT. I'M ALRIGHT,' she gasped. 'NOTHING WRONG WITH ME.'

There was a beat of silence; then Crystal started to clap. Everyone else joined in. Liz realised they were all clapping for her, and blushed.

'Well done, Mrs McLuckie,' said Bob the barber.

'Thank you so much,' said Irwin. 'How did you know what to do?'

'I'm a nurse. Or used to be. The Heimlich manoeuvre's one of the first things they teach us.'

'Very well done.' Benedict patted Liz on the back.

Gregory heaved a sigh. 'Okay, people, now that drama's over, shall we get back to it?'

'I thought she was a goner there,' whispered Benedict as they made their way back to their seats.

'Me too,' said Liz.

In the middle of the crisis, as she'd hurried to Iris's aid, her heightened senses had registered there was one person watching more with interest than concern. The only person in the room who hadn't applauded afterwards. Deborah Grogan.

Gregory put an end to everyone's misery not long afterwards. In spite of her ordeal, Iris had been as loud as ever. Hoarse, but loud. The singers didn't hang around chatting as they usually did, but made their escape as quickly as they could. As Liz went to retrieve her coat, she realised Benedict was already nowhere to be seen. She assumed he'd either left, or was in the bathroom.

She buttoned up her coat and found her gloves in her pocket. Irwin was whispering animatedly to Gregory in a corner, and they were both quite red in the face. Iris, oblivious, was helping herself to what was left of the biscuits on the table. Her brush with death obviously hadn't affected her sweet tooth. Liz made her way out of the church.

To her surprise, Kevin was waiting in the porch.

'It's pouring down again out there. Dad walked here, so I thought I'd come to fetch him.'

'I thought he was gone already.'

Kevin shook his head. 'He hasn't come out yet. Can I give you a lift too?'

Liz was tempted, but decided against it. It was only a five-minute walk down the abbey steps, but a fifteen-minute drive

down Abbey Lane and back through the town. For her own
peace of mind, she didn't want to be in close proximity to
Benedict for any longer than she needed to be.

'It's okay, thanks. I don't mind getting wet.'

Kevin dropped his voice. 'The toxicology report is back on
Carolyn Grogan.'

'And?'

He shook his head.

Liz was taken aback. 'Nothing?'

'Nothing conclusive. No toxins, alcohol or drugs. There
were high levels of adrenaline, but that's usual with a heart
attack.'

'What about the mark on her neck?'

'It was so small, it could have been anything.'

But Liz wasn't so sure.

Her walk home down the steps was unpleasantly cold
and wet, but had the benefit of jump-starting her brain. Was
it possible to overdose on epinephrine? she wondered. Had
Carolyn been injected? That might or might not be possible,
but one thing was horribly clear, with no evidence of foul
play against Carolyn, there was no reason to think Neil had
been murdered either. Which put Mags right back in the
frame for negligence.

When she got back to the warmth of Gull Cottage, she
changed into her pyjamas, snuggled on the sofa with Nelson
and did an online search for epinephrine poisoning. She
discovered that an injection could have lethal effects,
resulting in tachycardia and hypertension. In other words, it
could induce a heart attack, with almost immediate effect.
She was curious – who exactly had been with Carolyn when
she died? She found her mobile phone and dialled. It rang a
few times before it was answered.

'*Hello?*'

'Hi, it's Liz McLuckie. I thought I'd give you a ring, to see how you were getting on.'

'Not great,' said Helen. 'Adam's locked himself away and won't talk to anyone. He's taken Carolyn's death really hard.'

'I thought they didn't get on?' Hadn't Deborah told her that none of her children had liked their stepmother?

There was a pause on the other end of the line. 'I wouldn't say that. Not exactly. I don't suppose it helped that she died in his arms.'

'Did she?' Liz was shocked.

'I was with Adam and Philip, in the foyer. Philip was fuming because Carolyn had gone to touch up her make-up when she should have been greeting people arriving from the church. Just after she came back, I thought she looked a bit peaky. I said are you okay, and she said fine. But then... she just grabbed her chest and keeled over. Adam grabbed her before she hit the floor. It was over in a matter of seconds. It was horrible. Just horrible. There was nothing we could do.'

'Awful.'

'Inspector Flint told us she'd questioned you about Dad's body.'

The change of subject tripped Liz momentarily. She hesitated before speaking. 'You can't fault her instinct on this one, can you? But at the end of the day, she has nothing concrete that connects me to it. Or you.'

'That's a relief.'

'Just sit tight and let it all blow over. If I don't see you before, have a merry Christmas.'

'You too.'

Liz hung up thoughtfully. The call hadn't really been much help. Adam, Helen and Philip had been with Carolyn when she died, but that didn't mean she couldn't have been injected by someone else just before that. The hotel had been packed with funeral guests. Anyone could have done it... yet... Liz scratched Nelson's ears absent-mindedly. Try as she might, she couldn't shake off the memory of Deborah's detached expression when Iris had been choking.

'So we're back to square one, then,' said Tilly the next day at the café.

'Looks that way,' agreed Liz. She cut the cheese toastie Mags had made her.

'I'm glad I never mentioned it to Mags. What can we do, Liz? There has to be something.'

Liz hesitated. 'I suppose I could ask Deborah to talk to Philip. Try to persuade him to drop the case.' Privately, she wasn't sure that would work. Not if Philip was as stubborn as his father. Not if Deborah—

'I heard an interesting rumour yesterday,' Tilly interrupted her thoughts. 'Philip Grogan's a gambler.'

'Really?'

'Carl Fraser from the arcades told Jessie in the post office that he sees him in the betting shop on Baxtergate most days.'

'I suppose if he has debts, that would be motive for murder.'

'But surely he would have killed Carolyn first, then Neil? To be sure of inheriting?'

'Not necessarily. Apparently she has no—'

She was going to say 'family', but was interrupted by someone crashing in through the café door. It was Kevin, pink-faced and panic-stricken.

'Where's Mags?' he gasped.

'In the kitchen,' said Tilly. 'Why?'

'Flint's on her way. She's going to arrest her for murder!'

20

'I 'm surprised it didn't happen sooner.' Mags dropped her coat onto a chair. 'It was just a matter of time.'

'Why?' said Liz. 'I don't understand.'

Kevin frowned at Liz. 'I'm as much in the dark as you are.' He turned to Mags. 'Bill Williams tipped me off that Flint had been looking at your juvenile records. What did she find?'

Tilly and Mags exchanged a look. Then Mags spoke.

'I was convicted for poisoning someone.'

Kevin looked as if he'd been struck by lightning.

Mags shrugged apologetically. 'That's what I was in the Young Offenders for.'

Kevin glared at Tilly. 'You knew?'

'Of course I did.'

'And you didn't think you should mention it to me? Neither of you?'

'We hoped it wouldn't come to that,' said Mags.

'You hoped it wouldn't...' Kevin tailed off, at a loss for words, and ran a hand through his hair. Just then, they heard the sound of a car on the street outside, and blue lights strobed through the window.

'Go out the back door.' Tilly pushed Kevin towards the kitchen. 'You don't want Flint to see you here. She'll know you've tipped us off.'

Kevin gave them all one final despairing look and fled through the beaded curtain.

Liz wanted to reassure Mags. 'Your previous conviction doesn't mean anything. It won't be admissible in court.'

'Yes, but it's given Flint a reason to look more closely. And now she has her teeth in me, I can't imagine she's going to let go.'

'But you have no *motive* for killing Grogan,' said Liz.

Tilly shrugged. 'Even if Flint can't get a murder charge to stick, she'll charge her with criminal negligence at the very least.'

'But she still needs *proof*,' insisted Liz. 'And she can't find something that isn't there.'

'I wish that were true.' Tilly looked bleak. 'But prison's full of people who know better.'

They heard car doors slamming, and moments later Flint strode into the café. The three women looked at her wearily.

'Margaret Mary Blunt, I'm arresting you on suspicion of murder.' Flint paused for a moment, clearly disappointed by their lack of reaction. 'You do not have to say anything. But, it may harm your defence if you do not mention when questioned something which you later rely on in court. Anything you do say may be given in evidence.'

'Whatever,' muttered Mags.

Tilly hugged her. 'I'll get you a solicitor. We'll get you out on bail.'

Mags nodded. 'Bye, Liz.' She grabbed her coat and turned to Flint. 'Let's go.'

Flint's face registered her disappointment. Perhaps she'd expected Mags to make a run for it? She'd probably hoped for some kind of resistance, verbal or physical. She had a deflated air as she led Mags outside.

Tilly and Liz watched through the window as they got into the squad car. PC Williams was driving, but he was careful not to meet their eyes.

When they'd gone, Tilly's face crumpled. She burst into tears. Liz put her arms around her. When her sobs had subsided, she patted her on the back.

'First things first,' she said. 'Get on the phone and find that solicitor you promised her, then go and pack your things.'

'But—'

'I'm not leaving you here on your own. It won't hurt to close the café for a couple of days.'

Tilly nodded and wiped her eyes. 'We have no customers anyway.'

Liz didn't voice her next thought – even if they had, that would change as soon as the news of Mags's arrest got out.

'So DO you want to tell me about it? I can't imagine Mags poisoning anyone.'

Tilly wrapped her fingers around her mug of hot chocolate and sighed. Her nose was red from crying, and she had mascara streaked down one of her cheeks. Nelson, sensing her distress, pushed his head onto her knee. Tilly stroked him absent-mindedly.

'I'm not sure where to start.'

Liz didn't push it, but waited for Tilly to continue.

Tilly sighed. 'Mags was only sixteen. She had a crush on someone at school. You know Mags is into witchy stuff? White magic and Tarot cards?'

Liz nodded. Mags had always been interested in that kind of thing. She'd stocked the shop in the café with books on horoscopes and rune reading, crystal balls and smudging sticks. Liz wondered where on earth this was going.

'Anyway,' continued Tilly, 'she was really smitten by this girl and decided she could do with some help. Supernatural help. She found a recipe for a love potion. Very old. Mostly it was harmless stuff... moon-cleansed water, powdered rose quartz, that kind of thing... but it also had a couple of foxglove petals in it.'

Now Liz could see where things were headed.

'Mags had no idea digitalis was poisonous. It wouldn't have been fatal – it probably wouldn't have had an effect at all – but the children's panel didn't see it that way. Mags had already been in and out of foster homes. She had a reputation as a runner. In the end I think it just boiled down to convenience.'

'Somewhere to put her.'

'Exactly. But it almost broke her.' Tilly sniffed and wiped her eyes. 'You know Mags. She's nothing like me. She doesn't give much away. But in spite of everything, she's an innocent at heart.' Tilly gave a shaky laugh. 'Deep down, I think she still believes in unicorns. I can't let her go back to prison.'

Liz nodded. 'For what it's worth, I don't think it'll come to that. There's no evidence Neil Grogan was poisoned deliberately. Not by Mags or anyone else. Just as importantly, Mags has no motive to kill him. The worst they can do is charge her with negligence.'

'You think they'll release her on bail?'

Liz nodded. 'I do.' She patted Tilly's hand. 'Try not to worry. Flint has nothing.'

'IN HIS STATEMENT, Mr Ossett says that you helped him empty the van that night.' Flint's hard eyes fixed on Liz. They were in one of the interview rooms at the police station. DC Williams was taking notes.

Liz nodded. '*Commander* Ossett and I took all the party food into his house.'

'Did you notice anything unusual?'

'Well...' Liz thought about it. 'There was a bag there. Someone's evening bag. Mags or Tilly had picked it up accidentally.'

'I'm not interested in petty thievery.'

Liz blinked. That was an outrageous thing to say, even by Flint's standards, but she bit back a retort. When she agreed to the interview, she'd decided that complete co-operation was the only sensible strategy. The sooner Flint could see she had no real evidence against Mags, the sooner she would let her go. Theoretically.

'No. There was nothing unusual about the food.'

'And when did Mr Ossett discover the sesame oil?'

'After we'd taken everything into the house.' She was pretty certain Benedict would have answered that question in his own statement.

'How many bottles of sauce and oils were there?'

'I don't know exactly. About half a dozen?'

'And what made him pick up that particular bottle?'

'I have no idea. You should ask him.' This time she couldn't help the comeback. Flint's questions were ridiculous.

'Do you have any reason to think Margaret Blunt had an axe to grind with the mayor?'

'An axe...?' Liz frowned. 'No. None at all. Why would she?'

Flint didn't answer, but a smile crept over her sharp features that gave Liz the chills. Flint stood up and smoothed her skirt. 'I have no more questions, for now. DC Williams will take a proper statement from you.' She nodded curtly to Williams and marched out of the room with a smirk.

Liz stared after her. That last question about Grogan had

wrong-footed her completely. Did Flint have something else on Mags? DC Williams shuffled his papers and picked up his pen. When he looked back at Liz, he flinched at her expression.

'Don't ask me anything,' he said. 'Please, Mrs Mac. I'm just here to take your statement.'

It took the best part of an hour. When she came out of the interview room, Liz realised she needed a pee, and headed into the ladies' toilets. She was washing her hands in the chipped sink when there was a knock at the door. The door opened, and Kevin's head appeared round it.

'There you are!' His face registered his relief. After a furtive peek behind him, he came in and shut the door.

'Sorry for the cloak and dagger,' he said. 'I can't be seen talking to you.'

'What the hell's going on?' demanded Liz.

'Neil Grogan used to sit on the council's children's panel. He sent Mags to the YOI.'

21

L iz had to pass the supermarket on the way home, so she stopped to buy a few necessities. Her brain wasn't working properly, and she wasn't in the mood for human interaction, so she paid for her purchases at the self-service till, dropped her change into her carrier bag, then walked slowly back to Gull Cottage.

For once the bustle of the little fishing town didn't raise her spirits. The sky looked heavy. The forecast was for possible snow, but not even the prospect of a white Christmas was enough to cheer her. The holiday wasn't shaping up to be a good one, white or otherwise.

When she got in, Tilly was taking something out of the oven. From the tantalising aroma, Liz guessed it was Tilly's speciality, lasagne. Nelson was so fast asleep in his basket he didn't even stir at the sound of Liz's key in the lock. She suspected a generous amount of minced meat had found its way into his stomach during Tilly's cooking process. Tilly juggled the hot dish onto the draining board with her oven mitts.

'Did you give Flint my love?' she said. 'I suppose it's only a matter of time before she drags me in as well.' She stripped the mitts off and looked at Liz properly for the first time.

'What?' she said. 'What's the matter?'

'I think you'd better sit down.'

After Liz had told Tilly about Grogan and the children's panel, they sat in silence at the table for quite a while.

'I feel a bit sick,' said Tilly eventually.

'I know what you mean.'

Tilly nodded at the lasagne. 'I don't think I can eat that.'

'Don't worry. We can warm it up later. I've bought wine.'

She found the bottles of wine she'd bought at the supermarket. They were so cold that the five-pound note that had been beside them in the carrier bag was soaking wet with condensation. Liz put it on the radiator, then poured them both a large glass of wine.

'Do you think Mags knew?' she asked.

Tilly took a gulp of wine and shook her head. 'If she did, she never mentioned it to me. And anyway... why hold a grudge all these years? We were happy. I don't think she would risk that.'

'I'm sure she wouldn't.'

'Besides,' continued Tilly, 'Grogan was only one of a panel of... how many?'

Liz shrugged. She had no idea.

'Why would she single him out more than anyone else?' Tilly shook her head. 'She didn't do it. It makes no sense.'

None of it made any sense. But... there was something nagging at the back of Liz's brain. Had she maybe seen something? Heard something? It didn't necessarily have to do with Mags and Grogan, but there was definitely something lurking there.

She noticed Tilly's glass was empty, and filled it up again from the bottle. She couldn't dismiss the feeling she was missing something.

Her phone rang.

'*Is this Liz McLuckie?*'

'Yes.'

'*My name is Keith Muggeridge. I'm an officer with the DDU.*'

'DDU?'

'*Dangerous Dog Unit. I need to make an assessment of your animal as soon as possible.*'

'There's really no hurry. Nelson isn't dangerous.'

'*As soon as possible.*'

Liz had to think fast. 'Actually, I'm going away for Christmas first thing in the morning. To Ireland.' She'd picked the destination out of thin air. 'I'll be taking Nelson with me.'

'*I don't think...*'

She interrupted him. 'But I'll be back the day after Boxing Day. Can we make an appointment then?'

There was a pause on the other end of the line. Liz guessed the DDU officer would be thinking about his own holiday arrangements. He probably also wanted to break for Christmas as soon as he could. And if Nelson wasn't on his patch, he wouldn't be his personal liability. Liz held her breath until he spoke again.

'*The twenty-seventh, then. Ten o'clock.*'

'Thank you. See you then,' said Liz brightly. She hung up and looked at Tilly, who'd been listening to the whole exchange. Then she burst into tears.

Tilly hugged her. 'Don't worry,' she soothed. 'When they meet him, they'll see he's just a big softy. And everyone knows what Dora's like.' She refilled Liz's glass and pressed it into her hand. 'Get this down you. Everything will look better in the morning.'

. . .

TILLY'S OPTIMISM WAS MISGUIDED. Liz woke the next morning to the sound of Nelson downstairs scratching to be let out. She sat up with a groan. A few glasses of wine would never have affected her when she was younger, no matter how generously poured, but now her mouth was dry, and there was a distinct throb behind her eyes. She pulled on some jeans and a jumper and made her way downstairs via the bathroom, where she found some painkillers.

In the kitchen Nelson greeted her, then scratched at the front door.

'I know, I know. Give me a minute.'

She ran a glass of water to take her tablets, and spotted the empty lasagne dish in the sink. She and Tilly had ended up eating it straight from the dish. She splashed some water into it, promising herself she'd wash it out properly when she was feeling better.

The snow hadn't materialised, but outside the air was bitterly cold. The sea lapped the stones on the beach sluggishly as she and Nelson walked along the shoreline opposite the quayside. Nelson had been disappointed not to be going up to the churchyard, but was now trotting over the pebbles, sniffing seaweed, and nosing into cracks in the rocks.

Liz took a deep breath. And then it hit her. She wasn't sure whether it was the painkillers kicking in or the freezing air clearing her head, but it came to her like a lightning bolt. The thing she'd seen but not really *seen*. *Of course.*

'Nelson!' she called. 'Come on. We have to get you home.'

SHE WAS RELIEVED to find that the *Bugle* hadn't already closed for the Christmas holidays. She supposed it was true that 'news never sleeps', even in a sleepy fishing town like Whitby. She paid her fee and settled into the cubicle. Because she knew what she was looking for, it took her less than two minutes to find it.

Star pupils awarded science prize.

The five Whitby Academy sixth-formers grinned out at her from the photograph. Carolyn Grogan held the science award aloft in one hand, while her other hand... Liz peered more closely at the photograph. Her hand was partly hidden in the folds of her skirt, but she was surreptitiously grasping something... the fingers of the boy standing next to her. That boy was Adam Grogan.

He hadn't really changed much, even though a dozen years had passed – he still had the same healthy glow and broad shoulders beneath his school blazer. Liz didn't know why she hadn't recognised him before. Perhaps it was because she'd been so focused on Dora's story? She hadn't registered Adam consciously, but her subconscious – bless it! – had taken note. If Carolyn and Adam had been boyfriend and girlfriend before she married his dad, that would put a completely new spin on things, wouldn't it? But first she needed confirmation. She used her phone to search the Whitby Academy website, but couldn't find what she was looking for. She dialled a number from her contacts list.

'Hi, Crystal. Sorry to bother you, I know school's broken up for the holidays, but I have a quick favour to ask.'

'Most photogenic couple?' Tilly stared at the photograph that showed Adam with his arm around Carolyn's shoulders in the 2009 Whitby Academy yearbook. Crystal had found it in the school library, and now Liz was showing it to Tilly and Kevin in her kitchen.

'It doesn't say how long they were going out together,' said Liz, 'but they were definitely an item.'

'He can't have been happy when she married his dad.' Kevin inspected the photograph thoughtfully. 'Having a step-mother is bad enough, but having one you used to date...' He shook his head.

Liz gave him a sideways look, distracted by his words. Did he really think it would be so awful to have a stepmother? Then she realised what she was thinking and gave herself a mental shake.

'Mags saw Adam in the museum kitchen the night Neil died,' she said.

'He could have swapped the oil,' said Tilly excitedly. 'And Carolyn could have tampered with the EpiPen, knowing she would have to use it! They could have killed him together!'

'Whoa! Hold your horses,' said Kevin. 'That's a huge assumption.'

'Even if they weren't still romantically involved,' said Liz, 'now we know Adam had a motive to kill Neil.'

'Do we? What about Carolyn?' Kevin was still dubious. 'Why would he kill her?'

'She could have been killed by someone else,' suggested Liz.

Kevin pulled a face. '*Two* murderers? I think we need to take a few steps back.' He tapped the yearbook photograph. 'This proves nothing.'

'But—' Tilly began.

'There's no proof that Adam and Carolyn were still involved with each other. No proof that anyone swapped the oil in the kitchen, or that the EpiPen was tampered with.'

Liz squared her shoulders. 'Then perhaps we should stop messing about and find some.'

22

L iz took a deep breath and closed her eyes. What she was about to do was risky – possibly even dangerous – but would be worth it if she could clear Mags's name. She opened her eyes again and went into the reception of Shapeshifters Gym. The foyer was busier than she had expected, with people coming and going, clutching sports bags and water bottles. It was ten o'clock, an hour when most people should have been at work, but Liz realised most people had already finished for the holidays. It was the day before Christmas Eve, after all.

The young woman behind the desk recognised her. Almost.

'Mrs McLacky, isn't it? Have you decided to join us after all?'

'Not today. I'd like to see Mr Grogan, please.'

The woman exchanged a look with a young man in shorts who was putting fresh towels on the shelves beside her.

'He's very busy,' she said. 'He's not seeing anyone just now.'

'I think he'll see me.' Liz pushed an envelope across the desk. 'If you give him that.'

The woman took the envelope and looked at it dubiously. It was clear she didn't want to deliver the note to Adam.

'Give it here,' said the young man. 'I'll do it.' He took the envelope and disappeared into the bowels of the building.

Liz didn't have to wait long before he was back again.

'This way.'

She followed him down a series of corridors that smelled of disinfectant, until they came to a wood-panelled door.

'Just knock and go in.' The young man hesitated. 'I should probably warn you... Mr Grogan is a bit... under the weather. He probably shouldn't be at work, but...'

'He's the boss, and no one's going to tell him that.'

He nodded, relieved he didn't have to spell it out. When he'd gone, Liz adjusted her bra, which was digging into her ribcage, took a deep breath and knocked.

There was no reply. She went in anyway.

It took a while for her eyes to adjust to the light. All the blinds were down, and the only illumination came from a desk lamp that was angled up at a Buddhist mandala on one of the walls. She guessed the room should have been luxurious, but it wasn't. There was a stained duvet on the sofa, and the polished wooden floor and designer rug were strewn with empty pizza boxes, takeaway cartons and cans. It smelled of stale food, sweat, and beer. There was music too – 'Nothing Compares 2 U' drifted from hidden speakers. Liz wasn't sure when it had been in the charts, but she could take an educated guess. 1990. The year Adam and Carolyn had been together.

At first she didn't see Adam, but she could feel the weight of his eyes. As her own eyes adjusted, she saw he was sitting in the chair behind the glass and leather desk. He'd changed. His hair and clothes were dishevelled, and his healthy glow had gone, replaced by stubble and hollow cheeks. How long had he been there? Liz wondered. Carolyn had been dead for almost a week.

'What's this?' He held up the photograph that Liz had photocopied from the yearbook.

'I thought you might like a souvenir.'

'A souvenir?' Adam snorted. He didn't sound as if he'd been drinking, but it was still early. Perhaps he hadn't started yet. 'What makes you think I want to be reminded?' He narrowed his eyes at Liz. 'What's it got to do with you, anyway?'

Liz moved closer to the desk. 'Let's just say I'm an interested party.' She looked around and shook her head. 'You've made quite a mess in here.' She picked up the waste bin and started putting food cartons into it. Then she went to the windows and tugged the cord of one of the blinds.

Adam winced and threw up a hand to shield his eyes.

'Stop!' he croaked. 'Just stop. Sit down.' He looked even worse in daylight, at least ten years older than when she'd last seen him at his father's funeral.

Liz sat. As they faced each other across the desk, Sinead O'Connor's haunting voice stopped... then started again. Adam was playing it on a loop. He stared at Liz. She guessed he was trying to size her up, to work out how much she knew. Attack was maybe the best form of defence?

'Why didn't you tell the police you and Carolyn had been together?' she demanded.

'Because it was ancient history. And none of their business.'

'But you were still in love with her?'

She wasn't able to see his reaction to that, because he stood up quickly and went to the fridge in the corner behind him. When he opened the door, she saw there were energy drinks and medical supplies inside, but it was mostly stacked with cans of beer. He took one out and opened it, dropping the ring pull onto the floor with dozens of others.

He took a slug of beer, wiped his mouth and gave a bitter laugh. 'They got married in the Seychelles. I hadn't seen her for years... And then there she was. My new stepmother.' He paced the floor.

Liz watched him carefully, knowing he could be lying. His father's marriage could have been set up right from the beginning, planned by him and Carolyn, but she had to admit his distress sounded genuine.

'We were together two years. Two years!'

'Neil knew?'

'Of course he knew. *Everyone* knew. Everyone knew she'd dumped me and broken my heart. Dad didn't give a toss. He wasn't exactly a model parent.' Adam dropped heavily back into his chair. 'Did you know I have a police record?'

Liz didn't respond, assuming it was a rhetorical question. Adam seemed to be on a roll, and she wanted him to keep going.

He took another slug from the can. 'When I was twelve, I was picked up by the police. The usual stuff. Shoplifting a CD. When the police called Dad, he refused to come and get me. He actually locked Mum in their bedroom to stop her from coming either. I stayed in the police cell all night. At twelve years old.'

Liz was shocked.

'After that, I promised myself I'd take nothing from him.' He swept his arm around the room. 'I built all this myself from nothing. Without him or his money.'

'And then he brought Carolyn home.'

Adam looked bleak, drained the can and tossed it onto the floor behind him. 'Every time he touched her, I wanted to kill him. I wanted to kill them both.'

His words hung in the air between them as he went to the

fridge to get another beer. When he came back, his eyes locked with Liz's. They were black with pain and grief... and guilt.

Liz needed him to spell it out.

'You killed them?'

Adam drained the can, then tossed it away. 'The old man died easily enough when it came down to it.'

'Because of the sesame allergy?' Liz hardly dared to breathe.

'I waited until the caterer was out of the kitchen; then I swapped her cooking oil. I knew nature would do the rest.'

'Nature and the EpiPen.'

Adam's eyes refocused on Liz, almost as if he'd forgotten she was there. 'What?'

'How did you know the EpiPen wouldn't work?'

Adam's eyes narrowed. He was back in the real world again. He pushed himself to his feet and approached Liz around the desk.

'Why are you so interested?'

Liz couldn't think of an answer.

Adam came closer until he was towering over her. 'Are you recording this?'

'What?'

'On your phone? Show it to me!'

Liz hesitated.

'Now!' he snarled. Liz realised she'd better do as he said. He was a man on the edge. She took her phone from her pocket and gave it to him.

He smiled when he saw she hadn't been recording. Liz tried to stand, but he shoved her back down again.

'Who do you think you are? Coming in here, throwing accusations around?'

'I'm just —' Liz stammered.

'You shouldn't poke your nose into other people's business.' He jabbed his finger into Liz's chest. 'It's dangerous.' He gave a harsh laugh. 'It might even get you killed.'

He broke off and swung round at the sound of boots pounding down the corridor outside. The door burst open as Kevin, DC Williams and two more policemen shouldered their way in. Adam gaped. Williams took advantage of his surprise to grab his arms and force them behind his back. Liz heard the click of handcuffs.

She tried to stand but couldn't. Her legs were too weak.

Kevin squared up to Adam and glared. 'Adam Grogan, I'm arresting you for the murder of your father, Neil Grogan. You do not have to say anything, but it may harm your defence if you do not mention when questioned something which you later rely on in court. Anything you do say may be given in evidence.'

Adam said nothing and hung his head. His whole demeanour had changed from the murderous bully of a few moments before to a defeated boy. Kevin signalled for Williams to take him out. The other male officer followed.

'We'd better get forensics in here,' Kevin said to the remaining female officer. 'Go through everything.' He turned to Liz. 'Are you okay?'

'I'm not sure. I can't feel my legs.'

'Let's get that lot off you. Fletcher, give her a hand, will you?' He turned his back while the female officer helped Liz remove her jumper and tee shirt and take off the wire that was taped to her chest. Liz adjusted her bra and got dressed again. The female officer went out with the equipment, leaving Kevin and Liz alone. It had been Liz's idea to confront Adam directly, but it had taken a lot of persuasion to get Kevin on board. In the end he had only agreed on condition she wear a wire, and that he and his team station themselves nearby.

'Will any of that stand up in court?' asked Liz.

Kevin shrugged. 'Possibly not. But I think we'll get a confession anyway.' He looked around the room and pulled a face. 'What a mess. Has he been in here ever since she died?'

'I think so.'

Kevin prodded one of the empty beer cans with his toe. 'I suppose that's what a guilty conscience does for you.'

'I suppose.'

Kevin caught her tone. He gave her a quizzical look.

'He said he killed Neil, but he didn't say anything about Carolyn,' Liz said. 'Adam has a guilty conscience, but the question is... is it just for killing his father, or is there something else too?'

23

'Shhh. They're here!' hissed Liz.

'ALREADY? BUT—' Iris's observation was cut short by Irwin, who clapped a hand over her mouth. They all waited in the darkness as they heard Tilly's key in the back door. A light came on in the kitchen beyond the beaded curtain. Irwin released Iris and put his finger to his lips. Iris nodded and beamed.

After a few moments, Mags pushed her way through the curtain and switched on the café lights.

'SURPRISE!'

Mags gasped. Everyone was there: Liz, Benedict and Kevin, Iris and Irwin, Grazyna, Eryk and Lukasz, and Nelson. They all cheered apart from Nelson, who gave his plastic pig an emphatic SQUEAK. Eryk pulled a party popper, filling the air with coloured paper.

'Welcome home,' said Benedict.

'Thank you.'

'Come and have some champagne,' commanded Grazyna. 'Kevin, open that bottle right now.'

Kevin hurried to obey. The cork went off with a loud POP, and he filled the waiting glasses on the counter.

'Let's put the Christmas lights on!' squealed Lukasz.

'I want to do it!' shouted Eryk. The two boys squabbled their way to the tree.

Tilly put her arm around a still-motionless Mags.

'Was this your idea?' asked Mags.

'It was everyone's. We're just glad to have you home.'

'HOME FOR CHRISTMAS!' bellowed Iris.

Mags had only just made it. Her solicitor had pulled out all the stops to have her released as soon as Adam had been arrested, but in spite of all their efforts, she'd still ended up having to spend one more night in the cells.

But now it was Christmas Eve, and she was home.

Irwin gave Mags a brimming glass. 'Bottoms up!'

'It's a bit early for booze, isn't it?' said Mags.

'Nonsense,' said Irwin. 'Any time is champagne-o'clock. And this morning, we really have something to celebrate.'

'I've made mulled wine for later too,' said Liz.

'I thought you didn't like mulled wine?' said Mags.

Liz laughed. 'I don't. Normally. But this is made to your recipe, so I might give it another try.'

'We have sausage rolls,' crowed Lukasz, 'and what's these things again, Mum?'

'Vol au vents,' said Grazyna.

'And vollyvents!'

'And Christmas cake and mince pies!' yelled Eryk, not to be outdone.

Tilly pulled out a chair for Mags to sit down. She looked at all her friends with tears in her eyes. 'Thank you so much, everyone. Not just for this... for having faith. For sticking by me.' Her eyes sought Liz's, and she lifted her glass in a silent and specific salute. Liz lifted her own glass and grinned.

'WE KNEW YOU WEREN'T A POISONER, DIDN'T WE, IRWIN?'

Liz took in the scene in front of her, the café twinkling with lights and all her friends gathered together, and felt her own eyes prickle. She blinked back tears of gratitude.

'I'm beginning to think you have a death wish,' said Benedict, in her ear.

She turned to smile up at him. 'Really?'

'What made you take such a risk?'

Liz turned to look at everyone else. They were all laughing, chattering and sipping champagne. 'Isn't it obvious?'

'All's well that ends well, I suppose?' said Benedict.

'Definitely.'

Liz sipped her own champagne. She had invited Gillian to join them too, but she had made her excuses – it was Christmas Eve, one of her busiest days of the year. Liz realised there was someone else who wasn't joining in the fun either – Kevin was leaning on the counter, watching everyone but not really participating. Liz frowned.

'These mince pies are heaven,' said Mags. 'Please tell me they're not shop-bought.'

'Benedict made them,' said Tilly.

'What's your recipe?' Mags patted the seat beside her for Benedict to sit beside her.

Liz sidled up to Kevin.

'Can I ask you a personal question?' she said, keeping her voice low.

'I don't know.' Kevin's tone was wry. 'Is it possible to stop you?'

Liz grinned. 'Did you break up with Anna, or did she break up with you?'

'Neither. It just fizzled out.'

'Fizzled out how?'

'We said we'd arrange another date. I texted her, but she didn't get back to me.'

'Couldn't she have just been busy?'

'We're both busy. That's the problem.' Kevin shrugged. 'I don't want to force myself on her.'

Liz bit back a groan. 'Surely it isn't a question of *forcing*?' she said. 'It's just about finding out what's actually going on from her point of view.'

'How do you mean?'

Liz sighed. 'Okay. Imagine she was really, really busy when she got your text. She intended to answer it, but things got in the way. You know what it's like.'

Kevin nodded. He did.

Liz continued. 'A day passes. Then two days. When she gets the chance to respond, she realises it might be awkward to do it now. Are you even still interested? When she doesn't hear from you again, she decides you're not.'

'But *I* texted *her*.'

'Would it be so humiliating to text her again?'

Kevin hesitated.

'What do you have to lose? And it is Christmas, after all.'

Kevin nodded. 'You might be right.' He chinked his glass against hers. 'Merry Christmas.'

'*GOD REST YE MERRY GENTLEMEN, LET NOTHING YOU DISMAY!*'

Iris burst spontaneously into song on the other side of the room. Everyone joined in, singing as loudly as they could to be heard over her.

'*FOR JESUS CHRIST OUR SAVIOUR WAS BORN ON CHRISTMAS DAY!*'

AFTERWARDS, Liz took Nelson home, with a goodie bag of festive food. She wasn't sure whether she'd eat it before heading out to choir practice that afternoon, or later for supper before the carol service itself. Maybe both. Tilly had been generous.

She spent the early afternoon trying to relax, but found it hard after the excitement of the previous days. The undecorated cottage also deflated her mood. She wished – not for the first time – that she'd persevered in finding a tree after her debacle with Dora. Eventually she made herself a cosy spot on the sofa in the upstairs sitting room and curled up with Nelson. She'd just started to doze off when Nelson startled her by jumping up and clattering down the stairs.

YIP, YIP!

Liz followed, rubbing her eyes. There was definitely someone at the door, but they hadn't knocked. She wondered why not, until she heard the strains of a Christmas carol.

'Away in a manger, no crib for a bed
'The little lord Jesus laid down his sweet head.'

When she opened her door, she found three little girls warbling on her doorstep, dressed in pink and lilac knitwear, their faces pinched with cold. A woman – their mother, Liz assumed – watched them from the other side of the street, hopping from foot to foot to keep warm.

When they came to the end of the carol, Liz realised with dismay that she had nothing to give them. She had no cash in her purse. But then she remembered the five-pound note she'd put on the radiator. She ducked into the cottage to grab it.

'Lovely singing. Thank you.' She pressed it into one of their mittened hands.

'Thanks.' The woman nodded and smiled at Liz over the girls' heads. 'Come on, you lot. Home.' She cast an anxious glance up at the sky. It was heavy, a sullen yellow cast to it. Definitely looked like snow. She took the banknote from her daughter. 'I'll keep that safe, Lily.' Then she paused and approached Liz.

'Sorry, you gave her this too by mistake.'

It was just the supermarket till receipt that must have been crumpled up with the banknote when she'd put it on the radiator to dry. Liz took it from her.

'Thanks. Merry Christmas.'

'Merry Christmas!' chimed the girls.

Liz went back inside. She went to put the receipt in the bin and paused, looking down at it. Like the five-pound note, it had obviously been wet with condensation from contact with the wine bottle. The ink had smudged, making it illegible. What did it remind her of? The taxi receipt she'd found in the mystery bag. That made Liz wonder – had *it* been next to something cold in the handbag? What on earth would someone have taken to the museum party that could have been so cold? It came to her in a flash. Anna had told her that adrenaline breaks down at cold temperatures. Had Carolyn chilled, or even frozen, the EpiPen before putting it in her bag? No one had ever claimed the handbag, but Liz was now willing to bet it was Carolyn's.

She remembered how Adam had turned on her when she'd mentioned the EpiPen. Was he trying to protect Carolyn? Had she been in on it right from the start, after all? If so, who had killed her? Adam? That didn't seem to make sense. Of course, there was always the possibility that no one had killed her. It could have been a simple heart attack, like the coroner had said.

Liz sighed. Mags was in the clear. It was really none of her business now. Plus, it was almost Christmas, and she had other things to think about.

24

'It's no good,' muttered Gregory. 'We can't do it.'

Liz shivered in the chill air of the vestry. They'd just finished their final choir practice, and it had been just as much of a disaster as the others – worse even than Neil Grogan's funeral. She'd come to look for Gillian while everyone was putting on their coats, and had found her and Gregory in urgent, clandestine discussion.

'But surely,' soothed Gillian, 'it isn't about the quality of the singing. It's about the celebration of Christ's birth?'

Gregory gave her an offended look. 'I'm a *choirmaster*. Of course it's about the quality of the singing. It's *all* about that.'

Gillian sighed. 'What do you think, Liz?'

'It would be a pity for the singers, but I have to admit, I can see Gregory's point. We sound awful.'

'You see?' said Gregory. 'I'd never be able to show my face again.'

Gillian heaved a sigh. 'Well, I suppose we'll just have the congregation singing, then.'

'How are you going to stop Iris from joining in?' asked Gregory.

'We can't,' said Gillian. 'But I wouldn't want to. Are you quite sure you won't do the carol service?'

Gregory nodded. 'Sorry, Reverend, but I've made up my mind.'

'Okay.' Gillian lifted her hands in surrender and frustration. 'You'd better go and tell them, then.'

They headed out of the vestry together.

Gregory cleared his throat. 'Can I have a word, everyone?'

The singers, who were all at various stages of putting on their coats and packing their music away, turned to look at him.

'I've just been talking to the reverend, and we've agreed... the Eskside Singers won't be singing at the service tonight. We're just not ready.'

There were no protestations or groans of disbelief. Most people looked relieved – except for one.

'I THOUGHT WE SOUNDED GREAT. WE SOUNDED GREAT, DIDN'T WE, IRWIN?'

Irwin loved his mum, but even he couldn't bring himself to tell such a blatant lie. He just looked hard at Gregory.

'I'm sorry.' Gregory had the grace to look a little ashamed. 'I'll be in touch to let you know when our first meeting will be in the new year.'

'Will it be back down at the church hall?' asked Crystal.

Gregory nodded. 'Back at the church hall.'

People began to file out.

'Thank heavens for that,' muttered Deborah Grogan to Liz. 'Talk about a last-minute reprieve.'

Everyone had been surprised to see Deborah at the rehearsal, considering her husband had just died and her son was arrested for his murder, but Liz supposed she needed the distraction. She looked as composed and well put together as ever, in a tweed skirt suit and dark red lipstick.

Dark red lipstick?

'I DON'T UNDERSTAND IT.' Iris broke into Liz's thoughts. 'I WAS REALLY LOOKING FORWARD TO TONIGHT.' The old lady looked bewildered.

'We all were,' lied Benedict. He patted Iris on the shoulder. 'We all were.'

'Come on, Mother,' said Irwin, 'let's find your coat.' He steered her to the coat rack. Benedict caught Liz's eye.

'For what it's worth,' he muttered, 'I think Gregory's out of order. What does it matter what we sound like?'

'Mm.' Liz was noncommittal. She'd wanted Gregory to cancel, but now she felt bad about it. She felt mean. Perhaps Benedict was right?

'I'll see you here tonight anyway?' Benedict asked.

She wasn't sure she could be bothered if it was just an ordinary carol service. She didn't usually go to church. 'I might.'

He nodded. 'I'll leave the Merry Christmases 'til later, then.'

He headed for his car in the car park. Liz walked slowly down the abbey steps with Iris and Irwin. Even though it wasn't yet three o'clock, it was gloomy. They had to make their way down with care.

'WHY DO YOU THINK HE'S CANCELLED? DO YOU SUPPOSE IT WAS BECAUSE OF DEBORAH GROGAN'S PIANO PLAYING? SHE HIT A FEW BUM NOTES BACK THERE.'

'Did she?' Irwin looked doubtful. 'I suppose her mind's on other things.' Liz said nothing. *Dark red lipstick. Chanel Rouge Noir?*

'I was thinking of taking a quick walk on the beach,' said Irwin. 'Do you think Nelson would like to come?'

Liz was jerked from her thoughts. 'That's really kind. I'm sure he'd love to.'

'Can I pick him up now?'

'Yes.' Liz revised that. 'No.' She realised she was making no sense. 'Actually, there's something I have to do just now, really, really quickly.' Then she remembered she still had the spare keys she'd had cut for Tilly in her pocket. 'You can pop in and get him if you like?' She gave him the keys.

'As long as you're sure?'

'Very sure. He needs a decent walk. Thank you so much.'

Liz took out her phone as soon as she left them at the bottom of the steps.

'Helen. Hi.'

You have a nerve.

'Sorry?'

'If it weren't for you, the police wouldn't have jumped to ridiculous conclusions and arrested Adam.'

Liz realised she'd made a mistake calling her. 'I'm sorry.'

'You should be.' Helen hung up.

Ouch. Liz had been so focused on talking to someone who'd been at the museum party that she'd been hasty and insensitive. Helen was clearly the wrong person to ask. She would have to try plan B.

Dora took a long time to open her door. Liz could hear the sound of bolts being pulled back and chains being unhooked. Dora opened the door in her plaid dressing gown with curlers in her hair, clearly settled in for the afternoon. She was surprised to see Liz.

'What do you want? If this is about that dog of yours...'

Liz cut her off. 'It isn't. I just have a very, very quick question. Did you take any photos at the museum Christmas party?'

Dora was taken aback. 'Photos? I'm not some teenager taking selfies all the time, you know.'

'Of course not.' Liz changed tack. 'I don't suppose you can remember what Deborah Grogan was wearing?'

'As a matter of fact I do. I thought she looked like a stick of celery. A fat stick of celery. More like broccoli, actually.'

'Her dress was green?'

'Didn't I say that?' snapped Dora.

'Thank you.'

'Is that all?'

Liz hesitated. 'Not quite. I was wondering if you were coming to the carol service tonight.' By Dora's state of undress, Liz guessed that she probably wasn't, but pressed on. 'I'm sure everyone would love to see you there.'

'They would?'

'Definitely.'

As Liz made her escape, she heard the sound of Dora's door being locked again. She hoped that Dora would come. It would give her a proper opportunity to ask her to retract her accusations against Nelson. And besides, no one should have to spend Christmas Eve on their own. Not even Dora.

When Liz got back onto Church Street, the first flakes of snow were drifting down from the sky, falling on the cobbles like a dusting of icing sugar. Liz stopped under the Victorian-style lamp post in front of the Duke of York. She could hear the people inside the pub chatting and laughing, already making merry. She wondered what she should do next. She supposed she should find Kevin and tell him her suspicions about Deborah Grogan, but she had to admit, the evidence was tenuous – the blurred taxi receipt in the green evening bag and the Chanel Rouge Noir lipstick were hardly a smoking gun. Even if the bag was Deborah's, there could be a million ways the taxi receipt had blurred; it didn't have to be because it had been next to a chilled EpiPen. Yet... Liz had a feeling she was on the right track. It made sense that Adam had been working with an accomplice, someone who had tampered with Carolyn's EpiPen to make sure it wouldn't work. Either Carolyn herself... or... surely no one made more sense than Deborah? Deborah must have been humiliated by her husband's second marriage, and she'd have known how hurt Adam was. Did she help Adam kill his father? Did she then also kill Carolyn for good measure? *Hell hath no fury like a woman scorned.*

Yet Deborah had told Liz her marriage was already over when Neil and Carolyn had got together, and seemed quite relaxed about it. And there was also the business with Dora and her necklace. Deborah had tried her best to persuade Neil to return it. Poor Dora. The necklace had been all she had left of her mother and grandmother. Liz thought about the photograph of the beautiful woman in the high-necked dress. As she did, her eyes opened wider. She'd seen that necklace before.

To her relief, the Museum of Whitby Jet was still open. Liz could tell from the chatter and music farther back in the building that the restaurant was busy, but there was no one in the corridor to the shop. Everyone had finished their Christmas shopping.

Deborah's assistant Leah was on her own, tidying up.

'Oh, I'm sorry,' she said, 'we're closing at three today.'

'That's okay. I just want a quick look at one of your exhibits. I'll only be a minute.'

The girl hesitated, then nodded for Liz to go through.

She quickly found the display case she was looking for, the one with the collection of sea-themed pieces. She recognised the anchor brooch she'd noticed on her earlier visit, but it was the piece next to it that really held her attention. It was a necklace with a cameo pendant showing a carved arrangement of seashells and lilies. She hadn't taken much notice of it the first time she'd seen it, but that had been before she'd seen Dora's photograph. She looked at it hard. It was definitely Dora's necklace. Liz leaned to peer at the museum label beside it.

'What are you doing here?'

Liz snapped guiltily to attention. Helen frowned at her, her expression at odds with the jolly Christmas jumper she was wearing – Rudolph, complete with red pom-pom nose.

'I'm just...' stammered Liz. 'Just...'

'We're closing now.' Helen turned on her heel and headed back into the shop. Liz followed.

'It's okay, Leah,' said Helen. 'I'll lock up for Mrs Grogan. You can get on.'

The girl grinned. 'Thank you!' As she hurried out to whatever Christmas Eve celebrations she had planned, Liz started to follow her.

'Liz, wait.' Helen called her back. Her expression had thawed. 'I'm sorry. I'm sorry I was so rude to you on the phone, especially after everything you've done...' She shook her head, and her eyes filled with tears. 'It's just... Adam... it was such a shock.'

'I'm sorry too.' She genuinely was. But she also felt horribly guilty. If she was right about Deborah, Helen was going to lose her mum as well as her father and brother.

'How did you know?' asked Helen.

'Sorry?'

'How did you know it was Adam?'

'Mags saw him in the kitchen at the museum; then when I found out about him and Carolyn, I just put two and two together.'

'Really?' Helen shook her head in disbelief. 'He was devastated when Dad suddenly turned up with her like that... but we never thought... I never thought... well I suppose we never imagined he could do such a thing. Not on his own.'

Liz saw that Helen was watching her closely. Was she fishing? Perhaps she had suspicions about Deborah too?

'No,' said Liz. 'It did seem out of character.'

Helen wiped her eyes and sniffed. 'I suppose love makes fools of us all.'

'Or murderers.' Too late, Liz realised that sounded heartless. She smiled at Helen in an attempt to soften her words. Helen flashed her an uncertain look.

'Do you mind hanging on for a minute to watch the shop before I lock up?' she asked. She dabbed at her eyes. 'I need to freshen up.'

'Of course. Go ahead.'

'I won't be a minute. Can you put the lights off?'

As Helen disappeared in the direction of the ladies', Liz went to the light switches at the archway leading into the museum. Liz paused before putting the lights off. She wanted one last look at Dora's necklace. She went into the first exhibition room and studied it in the display case. Without the context of Dora's photograph, it was just another necklace – beautifully carved, but nothing extraordinary. It was the context of Dora's family history that made it special. Special only to Dora. Liz sighed. Even if she was right about Deborah, and Kevin could find the evidence to prove it, Dora was never likely to get her necklace back now. Liz bent to read the label.

Carved by Isaac Greenbury, circa 1851. Donated to the museum by Mrs H. M. Ricci.

25

'D o you like my necklace?'

Liz jumped. That had been fast.

'*Your* necklace?'

Helen nodded. 'Isaac Greenbury exhibited at the Great Exhibition. There aren't many pieces of his work left now. Dad gave it to me.'

So that was why Neil had refused to give it back to Dora. Liz noticed that Helen had reapplied her make-up. Her dark red lipstick made her mouth look larger than usual, but made her other features look harder.

Alarm bells rang in Liz's head. 'Just as a matter of interest,' she said, trying to make her tone as casual as possible, 'did you lose a bag at the museum party?'

'I did! I've been meaning to call the museum about it, but what with Dad and then everything else, it kept slipping my mind. Why do you ask?'

'The police have it.'

'The police?' Helen frowned.

'In lost property.'

'Ah.' Helen looked relieved. 'I'm glad. It's the only bag I have that goes with my emerald dress.'

Liz's head was whirling. Had she been on the wrong track? She followed Helen back through to the shop.

'Can I ask you something?' She knew she would have to be careful. 'You thought Carolyn had killed your dad, didn't you?'

'I thought *somebody* had, and she was the obvious suspect. She was going to get all his money.'

'Unless there was no body.'

'Sorry?'

'Even with a death certificate, if your father's body had gone missing, his estate would have been frozen. No insurer was likely to pay out either. Not for a long time.'

'I suppose.'

A silence hung between them.

'Was that why you took it?'

'What do you mean?'

'It had nothing to do with wanting another autopsy, did it?' Liz knew she was in deep now, but there was no going back. 'You just didn't want Carolyn to get the money.'

'She was a pathetic little gold digger.' Helen spat the last word as if it were poison. Her usually pleasant features had twisted with scorn. 'She and Adam were much better suited.'

'But she didn't want him. Even when Neil was dead.'

Helen picked up her bag and went to the shop door. 'Adam was devastated... Again... It upset our plan. I had to make a new one.'

Helen shot the bolts at the top and bottom of the door and turned the key in the lock. As she turned back to face Liz, she dropped the keys into her bag and took out something else.

A syringe.

'My new best friend,' she said, with a smile.

Liz glanced over her shoulder. The wall between the shop and the restaurant was glass, but although she could see through into the restaurant beyond, the tables were quite some way away, and no one was looking in their direction. Helen was much younger than Liz and, from what Liz had seen of her manhandling her father's corpse, stronger than she looked.

Liz's assessment of her situation took a fraction of a second. It didn't look good. She had to keep Helen talking.

'You killed Neil.'

Helen's lip curled. 'Technically, Adam did. I just stopped him from not dying. Adam swapped the oil, while I changed the EpiPen in Carolyn's bag for one I'd brought with me.'

'One you'd frozen.'

'Someone's been doing their homework.' She came towards Liz.

To hell with this. Liz made a dash to the glass wall and banged her fists on it.

'HELP!' She banged again. 'SOMEONE HELP ME!'

Nothing happened. No one stopped eating or even turned to look in her direction.

Helen smiled. 'Reinforced and soundproofed. The planners insisted.' She was still advancing on Liz, who was forced to retreat from the glass. Liz felt she'd stumbled into a nightmare. She was in mortal danger from a double murderer, and there were people sitting only yards away, oblivious. And it was Christmas Eve, for God's sake! Liz didn't know why that mattered, but it did. Helen's Rudolph jumper added to the atmosphere of unreality. His pom-pom nose held an absurd fascination for Liz as she backed away. She knew if Helen decided to make her move, she'd be done for.

'You injected Carolyn,' she said, buying time.

'My plan B? Yes, I did it in the ladies' loo at the hotel. It was easy.'

Liz nodded at the syringe. 'What's in there?'

'Adrenaline. Handy stuff. I always carry some with me now, just in case.'

Liz opened her mouth, then snapped it closed again. She'd almost said, 'You'll never get away with this.' Such a cliché. Pathetic. Without taking her eyes off Helen, she tried to gauge how far she was from the archway into the museum, which was behind her. It was a warren of rooms back there, and she had no idea if there was another way out – a back door or a fire exit. But it was worth a try. What choice did she have, anyway?

Liz darted for the archway, throwing a revolving display of earrings in Helen's path. As she bolted into the museum, she heard Helen's muttered expletive.

'Run if you like!' called Helen. 'There's no way out!'

Liz looked over her shoulder. Then... everything went black. Helen had turned off the lights.

'Shit!'

Liz crouched down and tried to steady her breathing. The shop lights were off too, so the only illumination was coming from the restaurant – the faintest glimmer of light through the archway back into the shop. Liz knew that the farther she went into the museum, the darker it would get. She thought about the phone in her pocket. Could she call Kevin? No – Helen would be on her too quickly. Using the torch wasn't an option, either. It would give away her position.

Helen held all the cards – she knew her way around, she was stronger than Liz, and she had the syringe. Liz tried to find courage by telling herself she'd been in worse situations before. But actually, she hadn't. She pushed herself to her feet.

Suddenly, someone grabbed her from behind. Helen must have circled round her! She hadn't heard a thing! As they grappled blindly together, Liz felt a sting on her neck.

The syringe! Somehow she found the strength she needed to elbow Helen away before she could press the plunger. Helen staggered back into the wall cabinets, which shattered, filling Liz's ears with the sound of breaking glass. She ran blindly in the direction of the next room, bouncing painfully off a wall before finding the archway and groping her way through it.

In the second room, Liz kept moving, with the instinct of a hunted animal, feeling her way in the darkness. It was pitch black now. In her head she tried to recreate the geography of the room from the last time she'd seen it. As far as she could remember, it was lined with wall displays the same as the first room, but also had free-standing cabinets in the middle. She crouched down, slowed her breathing and listened. She heard the faint sound of crunching glass. Helen was moving again. Did she still have the syringe, or had it been knocked out of her hand in their struggle? Liz had to assume she still had it.

Liz shuffled towards the middle of the room on her hands and knees. She stifled a cry as she bumped her head, and stood up, using the sides of the cabinet to climb to her feet. She felt her way around to the other side. The wood was smooth under Liz's fingers, and she could smell furniture polish. Liz tried to visualise the old-fashioned Victorian display case. How heavy was it likely to be? Hopefully not too heavy. She waited, breathing as quietly as she could, trying to calm the thudding of her heart.

She heard nothing. Maybe Helen was waiting for her to come out? It wasn't a bad strategy if, as Helen said, there was no exit at the back of the museum. Perhaps she had time to use her phone after all? She reached into her pocket.

But then she heard it, the softest exhalation. Helen was right there, on the other side of the cabinet! Liz took a deep breath and pushed with all her might. The cabinet was heavy and took every scrap of power she had to move it, but her own adrenaline lent her extra strength. It moved, then yielded. There was a cry of alarm as it toppled over with a crash.

Then there was silence.

Liz ran for the faintly illuminated archway into the first room. She careered through that room too, bouncing off the walls and crunching through broken glass until she found the bank of light switches at the door. She flipped them all on.

The light revealed devastation. Two of the wall cabinets had been smashed, and pieces of Jet lay scattered among the glass on the floor. Liz also saw a pair of shoes lying in the debris – Helen's navy sling-backs. She must have slipped them off to creep up on Liz. No wonder she hadn't heard her! Liz turned her attention to the room beyond. There was no sign of movement. No sound.

Liz fumbled for the phone in her pocket and dialled Kevin's number.

'Kevin!'

'Liz? Hi. What's the—'

'Come to the Whitby Jet Museum. Quickly! Bring help!'

She hung up and put the phone back in her pocket. There was still no noise or movement from the next room. She took a deep breath to steady herself, then went to look. There were smears of blood on the tiles leading away from the broken cabinets – Helen must have cut her bare feet on the broken glass. Liz followed the bloody trail into the next room.

The first thing Liz saw was the syringe, on the floor just inside the archway. She kicked it safely away.

Helen was lying on her side in the middle of the room, eyes closed, with her legs trapped under the toppled cabinet. There was blood on her forehead, and glass sparkled on her Rudolph jumper and in her hair. She wasn't moving. Liz couldn't see if she was breathing. She knelt down to check.

It took her a couple of moments to find the pulse under Helen's jaw, light but steady. She sighed with relief. For a second she thought she'd killed her. As wicked as Helen was, she didn't deserve to die. Liz grabbed her under the armpits and dragged her out from under the cabinet, then rolled her into the recovery position and made sure her airways were clear.

Back in the shop, nothing had changed apart from the fallen earring display stand. On the other side of the glass wall, people were still chatting and eating. Still oblivious. Liz shook her head in disbelief. She found the keys in Helen's bag to unlock the door.

Kevin arrived about six minutes later.

'Okay. Thanks, Bill. Let me know when her solicitor turns up.' Kevin hung up his phone and turned back to Liz. 'She's conscious, but saying nothing.'

Helen had been taken to hospital in an ambulance, accompanied by DC Williams.

'Do you know where she got the adrenaline?' asked Liz wearily. They'd been at the police station for hours.

'From the gym,' said Kevin. 'Adam was giving it to some of his clients to enhance their performance. Illegally of course. But he didn't know Helen had stolen some.'

'He's confessed?'

Kevin nodded. 'He held out for a while until Flint told him Helen had killed Carolyn. Then he told us everything. Helen helped him to kill Neil, but he swears he had no idea she was going to kill Carolyn too.'

'I believe him.' Liz looked at him over the interview room table. 'I think he'd have tried to stop her. He loved Carolyn.'

'But surely he must have guessed that Helen had done it?'

Liz shrugged. 'You'd think so, wouldn't you?'

'Is he a bit thick?'

Liz shook her head. 'He's bright enough. But perhaps he just didn't want to admit the truth.'

'He only saw what he wanted to see?'

'Don't we all?' Liz yawned. 'Can I go now?' She was so glad Irwin had her keys. She'd phoned him from the museum, and he'd told her it was no problem for him to look after Nelson for what was left of the day. In fact, he'd insisted.

'I don't see why not,' said Kevin. 'We have your statement, so...'

Liz's phone buzzed. Liz read the text and met Kevin's eyes. 'What now?' he asked. 'More drama?'

The text was from Benedict.

Come to St Mary's! The carol service is on!

She checked the time on her phone and was astonished to see it was five past eleven. She had no idea it was so late.

'It looks like the carol service is on again,' she said. 'I need to freshen up and get up there. Can you give me a lift?'

'No problem. We were planning on going anyway, before it was cancelled.'

'We?'

Kevin grinned. 'We can pick Anna up on the way.'

26

The interior of the church was atmospheric, with candlelight gleaming off the polished wooden box pews and the white barley-twist posts of the transept. Garlands of holly hung on the pews, and the altar was decorated with fir branches. It could have been a scene straight from the eighteen hundreds except for the panicking people. The Eskside Singers were all there, running around taking off their coats and trying to find their music.

'It's game on,' said Benedict to Liz when she got there.

'I don't understand,' said Liz. 'What made Gregory change his mind? Did Gillian persuade him?'

'Isn't it wonderful?' chirped Crystal, who had overheard their exchange. 'It's a Christmas miracle!' She hurried to the piano.

"What's she talking about?' Liz was confused.

Benedict grinned. 'You'll see.'

Gregory bustled out of the vestry. 'Come on, everyone! Coats off. Put them on the bench over there. Take your places. Everyone will be here soon.'

There were already a few members of the congregation in

the pews, people who'd driven choir members there. Kevin and Anna were among them, sitting towards the back. Kevin waved to them with his free hand. He had his other arm around Anna's shoulders.

Benedict spotted them. 'Is it on? Or off?' he whispered. 'I can't keep up.'

'On, obviously.' Liz smiled. 'Let's hope it stays that way.'

'Come on, Commander,' said Gregory. 'Get a move on. The gentlemen are waiting.'

Benedict hurried to join Irwin and the other tenors, beside the baritones.

More and more people were coming in now.

'Okay, everyone?' Gregory tapped his baton on his music stand. 'Let's give them all a gorgeous Christmas greeting. "O Holy Night".'

He waited for everyone to stop fidgeting and nodded to Crystal. Crystal thumped out the intro on the piano. Liz braced herself.

'O holy night, the stars are brightly shining,
'It is the night of the dear Saviour's birth...'

Everyone's eyes flew to Iris. Was she singing? Her mouth was opening and closing, but there was nothing coming out.

'Long lay the world in sin and error pining,
°Til he appeared and the soul felt its worth.'

There was still no sound coming from Iris. Everyone exchanged puzzled looks that changed to delight as they continued to sing.

'A thrill of hope the weary world rejoices,
'For yonder breaks a new and glorious morn.'

Liz glanced over her shoulder, looking for Irwin. What was going on? He caught her eye and winked. The singers launched into the chorus with gusto.

'Fall on your knees, Oh hear the angel voices!
'O night divine! O night when Christ was born.

'*O night, O holy night, O night divine.*'

As they sang, the congregation continued to arrive until all the pews were filled, and there were several rows of people standing at the back. The Christmas service was always the most well attended of the year, attracting folk who would never dream of coming any other time. Late as it was, there were quite a few children packed into the pews, rosy-faced with excitement, desperate to stay awake at all costs. Some hadn't succeeded and had fallen asleep in their parents' arms. Liz saw Tilly and Mags in the crowd and waved discreetly to them. She saw many other familiar faces too, including Grazyna and the boys, and Mike, the fishmonger, and his wife, but continued to scan the crowd until she found the one she was looking for. She spotted her hat first, in one of the back rows, just behind Kevin and Anna. The face under it was as sour as ever, but at least Dora was there. Liz was glad.

Gillian, resplendent in her most ornate vestments, opened her sermon from the topmost tier of the three-storey pulpit, with its carved canopy and red velvet hangings. Then the Eskside Singers led the congregation in their first carol.

'*Once in Royal David's city,*
'*Stood a lowly cattle shed...*'

Liz looked around the church as she sang. She wasn't a Christian. Although she'd grown up in a Methodist family, she'd ditched Sunday school as soon as she was old enough, and now only attended church for weddings and funerals – more of the latter than the former lately. Yet, as she sang the familiar lyrics of the hymn and looked around the candlelit church at the faces of the congregation, she felt something... gratitude? Hope? There were horrible people in the world like Helen Ricci, but they were outnumbered hundreds – thousands – to one. That thought made Liz happy, and feel very Christmassy indeed.

When the service was over, everyone with children

headed home to get them to bed, but most of the congregation stood around chattering and wishing each other Merry
Christmas. Liz made a beeline for Irwin and Iris.

'Iris! What happened? Are you okay?'

Iris pulled a face and pointed at her throat.

'She's fine,' said Irwin. 'She's just lost her voice. An
allergy. Had it for years, haven't you, Mother?' Irwin met Liz's
eye. 'Dogs.'

'Dogs?'

'Iris!' Benedict called to them from the pile of coats.
'What colour's yours? I'll get it for you.'

Not being able to answer, Iris went to show him.

Liz saw the gleam of mischief in Irwin's eyes.

'Nelson,' she said.

Irwin nodded. 'I took him to visit her this afternoon.' He
caught Liz's look.

'It wasn't deliberate. I'd forgotten she was allergic to
animal dander. I feel guilty, obviously,' he continued, not
looking guilty at all. 'But you have to admit, it's worked out
pretty well. It's an ill wind that blows no good.'

Liz had to admit that was true. 'She's going to want to
keep coming to the choir though, isn't she?'

'We'll jump that hurdle when we get to it. We need to
work on Gregory. Get him to loosen up a bit. Make him
realise it isn't the end of the world if we're not pitch-perfect.'
He took her keys from his pocket and gave them to her.
'Yours, I believe.'

'Thank you,' she said.

'You're very welcome.'

Iris returned to the group, carrying her coat.

'Have you got your hat and scarf?' asked Irwin. She
opened her mouth to speak, then remembered she couldn't.
She nodded vigorously instead and showed him the knitwear
she had in her hand. Liz had to look away. She found a silent

Iris a bit unnerving, if she was honest. She wasn't sure she liked it.

Benedict was talking to Gillian by the coats. They were standing close together, keeping their voices low so no one could hear what they were talking about. As Liz watched, Gillian smiled and put her hand on Benedict's arm. Were they friends again? Or more than friends? From their faces it was impossible to tell. Liz turned away. She couldn't bear to look.

'Look at you two lovebirds,' crowed Tilly. She was talking to Kevin and Anna, who'd also come to join them. They were holding hands. Anna blushed.

'I could say the same thing,' said Kevin, nodding at Tilly's and Mags's interlinked arms. The two women usually avoided public displays of affection, but tonight had thrown caution to the wind. It felt as if the spirit of peace and good-will had affected everyone. Lukasz and Eryk bounded up to their group, followed by Grazyna.

'Do you think Santa's been yet?' asked Lukasz.

'Has he, Mrs Mac?' demanded Eryk.

'I shouldn't think so,' said Liz. 'Not yet.'

Grazyna ruffled Eryk's hair. 'He does not come until children are fast asleep. And if they are bad children, he does not come at all.'

'We've been good, haven't we, Eryk?'

'We have! Honest!'

'Come on, Mum, let's go home.' Lukasz towed Grazyna towards the door. Eryk grabbed her other hand, and the two boys steered her out, like a tanker between tugboats.

'Are you still okay for the Boxing Day shift?' called Mags after her.

'I will be there!'

They all watched the boys drag her outside.

'She's back with you at the Full Moon, then?' asked Liz.

'Thank God,' said Mags. 'There's no need for her to stay at the Copper Kettle now.'

'She's part of the family,' said Tilly.

Everyone jumped as the bell in the belltower above them started to clang the hour. It wasn't the most melodious of church bells, but it was loud. It was chiming midnight.

'MERRY CHRISTMAS, EVERYBODY!' yelled Tilly.

'MERRY CHRISTMAS!' responded everyone except Iris, who just looked crestfallen, presumably because she couldn't join in. Liz gave her a hug. Over Iris's shoulder, she saw Dora heading out of the church. She kissed Iris on the cheek, then hurried to follow.

Snow had fallen all through the service, blanketing the clifftop, transforming the usually hard lines of its gravestones and stone walls into a magical wonderland. The other people who were coming out of the church at the same time as Liz 'oohed' and 'ahhed' at the sight, but Liz ran to catch up with her quarry, her feet crunching in the freshly fallen snow.

'Dora! Hang on.'

Dora didn't slow her stride. Liz eventually caught up with her at the top of the abbey steps.

'What is it?' snapped Dora.

'I'm glad you came,' said Liz breathlessly.

'Why should you care?'

'Because it's Christmas.' Dora's snarkiness failed to dent Liz's bonhomie. 'And I have a present for you.'

'Me?' Dora's face slackened with surprise.

Liz took the gift she had wrapped carefully in a piece of kitchen paper from her pocket, and gave it to Dora.

'Good to see you've gone to so much trouble,' sneered Dora. She unwrapped the paper and blinked in astonishment.

'Is this...?'

Liz nodded. 'Your grandmother's necklace.'

'It can't be.' Dora examined it minutely until she was convinced. 'How did you get it?' She looked at Liz accusingly. 'You didn't steal it, did you?'

'Of course not.'

That was exactly what she'd done. While she was waiting for Kevin to arrive at the museum, she'd searched through the debris of the broken display cabinets. Although much of the jewellery had come unstrung, and some had shattered completely, Dora's necklace was still intact. Liz hadn't felt the faintest flicker of guilt as she'd pocketed it. The Grogans didn't deserve it.

'It's yours,' she said to Dora. 'It always has been.'

Dora nodded and sniffed. 'As long as there won't be repercussions. The last thing I want is that Inspector Flint knocking at my door.'

'You'll be fine.' Liz was pretty certain that the necklace wouldn't be missed in the drama of the coming weeks. She hesitated before speaking again. 'I had a call from the Dangerous Dog Unit.'

Dora just looked at her.

Liz plunged on. 'It would be great... really great... if you could have a word with them. Tell them you were mistaken about Nelson.'

'Why would I do that?'

Liz resisted the urge to mention the necklace and shrugged instead. 'Because it's Christmas?' The church bells had finished chiming midnight, and were now ringing a jubilate that clanged through the clear night air. 'Merry Christmas, Dora.'

For a long moment Dora said nothing. Then she nodded.

'I'll see what I can do.' She turned and stomped off.

Liz watched the determined figure march away from her down the snowy steps. She was relieved and also a little peeved that Dora hadn't even wished her a Merry Christmas.

But Dora was Dora and always would be. In many ways she was her own worst enemy.

Liz hesitated. Should she go back into the church and finish wishing everyone Merry Christmas? She decided not to. She really didn't want to have to watch Gillian and Benedict together, and she would see most of her friends tomorrow anyway.

She followed Dora's example and set off down the steps herself, resisting the impulse to hurry, in case she slipped on the snowy stone. Home was calling. Nelson would be waiting for her in his basket in the warmth of Gull Cottage. His part in Irwin's Machiavellian plan might have been unwitting, but he still deserved a huge hug and maybe even one of his favourite treats. Liz grinned. Once again, the so-called ugliest dog in Yorkshire had saved the day, but this time nobody knew – not even him!

AUTHOR'S NOTE

Whitby is, of course, a real town – a historical gem of a fishing town on the North Yorkshire coast of the UK. It's famous as the birthplace of colonial explorer Captain Cook, and the inspiration for Bram Stoker's gothic masterpiece *Dracula*. Children adore it for its beaches, cobbled yards and alleyways and – of course – its ice cream and fish and chips.

I fell in love with Whitby on my very first visit, when I was five. It hasn't lost any of its charm for me in the intervening decades, and I still visit whenever I get the chance. I've tried to keep my fictional geography of the town as close to the real thing as possible. I may, however, have made a few mistakes and taken a couple of liberties, for which I hope you'll forgive me.

The Duke of York pub and the Captain Cook Memorial Museum on Grape Lane are both immensely popular with locals and tourists, for very different reasons. And, of course, the ruined abbey and St Mary's Church attract visitors from all over the world. I have tried to describe them as accurately as possible.

Kipper Cottage and Gull Cottage are based on the two

cottages closest to Fortune's Smokehouse, on Henrietta Street. The Full Moon Café and Shapeshifters Gym are my own invention.

Whitby Jet was wildly popular in the Victorian era, thanks to its adoption by the Queen herself, who, after the death of her consort Prince Albert, never wore anything but black. Isaac Greenbury was one of its most celebrated carvers and exhibited at the Great Exhibition of 1851. Not many examples of his work have survived. As well as the Museum of Whitby Jet, now luxuriously housed in the converted Wesley Chapel on Church Street alongside the excellent Albert's Eatery, there are many shops in the town that sell Jet jewellery, both new and antique.

I hope you've enjoyed spending time in Whitby with Liz McLuckie, and that you'll join her for her next adventure in the Kipper Cottage Mystery series.

Until then, happy armchair sleuthing!

If you'd care to leave a review on Amazon they are enormously helpful in getting books discovered by new readers and I would be grateful for you thoughts.

ABOUT THE AUTHOR

Jan lives just outside Edinburgh with her husband, three kids, a one-eye whippet and a fat black pug. Born in a colliery village in the North East of England, she cut her literary teeth on the great storytellers of the 60's and 70's - Wilbur Smith, Frank Yerby, Mary Renault, and Sergeanne Golon. She began her writing career as an advertising copywriter, and has since had novels published by Random House and HarperCollins, and original audio series produced by Audible UK. She also writes for tv.

Jan enjoys psychological thrillers and crime fiction of all kinds, from the coziest of cozies to the blackest of noirs.

You can find Jan at www.kippercottagemysteries.co.uk

ALSO BY JAN DURHAM

Kipper Cottage Mysteries

Death at the Abbey (Book 1)

Death at Neptune Yard (Book 2)

Death at the Feast (Book 3)

Death at the Anchorage (Book 4)

Death on the Stella Mae (Book 5)

Manufactured by Amazon.ca
Bolton, ON